SOUL GLAZE
THE DAHLIA WILDES MAGICAL MYSTERIES
BOOK IV

NOVA NELSON

FFS Media

Contents

Chapter 1	1
Chapter 2	15
Chapter 3	28
Chapter 4	40
Chapter 5	53
Chapter 6	58
Chapter 7	66
Chapter 8	75
Chapter 9	83
Chapter 10	90
Chapter 11	96
Chapter 12	102
Chapter 13	115
Chapter 14	130
Chapter 15	144
Chapter 16	154
Chapter 17	166
Chapter 18	170
Epilogue	174
About the Author	179
More books from Eastwind	181

Chapter One

Magical powers aren't all they're cracked up to be. When I first discovered I was a witch, the ability that worried me the most was seeing, hearing, and speaking to ghosts. It sounded terrifying, and in the months since acquiring my magic, I've certainly had some *interesting* ghost encounters. But as it turns out, that wasn't the trickiest of my powers to live with. The one making my legs feel like Jell-O as I strolled through downtown Eastwind on my day off was my power of Empathy.

I've always been an empathetic person—I never liked violent movies, even before I discovered my magic, because I couldn't handle the emotions—but this talent was something else entirely. As a Fifth Wind witch, I could sense people's emotions. I didn't do it on purpose, either. Waves of anger, sadness, or joy would hit me out of nowhere, like they were suddenly my own. Usually I could tell the difference, though, since my own moods

tended to be pretty even. I rarely got angry or jealous or…
Well, I didn't used to, anyway.

Since I'd moved to Eastwind—unwillingly, I might
add—emotions had become a much more vocal part of
my personality. It was unsettling, but undeniable. The
fact that I was letting more disruptive emotions through
only made it harder to tell where mine ended and other
people's began.

Nora Ashcroft, who had taken me under her wing,
insisted I learn to focus my emotional powers more
precisely. She saw it as a useful tool for solving mysteries
around Eastwind, and I could see her point. But from
where I stood, I couldn't imagine wanting to do more of it
than I already was. My own feelings were overwhelming
enough, and I'd have preferred to find a way to feel less
of them, not more.

The night before, Nora and I had wrapped up an
hour-long training session at her house, where Atlas and
I were staying. To say it left me exhausted would be
putting it mildly. My whole body, mind, and spirit felt
like mush this morning. I'd hoped a good night's sleep
would help, but my dreams had been vivid and chaotic,
so the exhaustion lingered as I made my way toward the
outskirts of town for a free breakfast—Nora's treat.

Atlas, walking beside me, was equally drained. Our
bond was growing stronger by the day, and after nearly
six months together, what tired me out seemed to tire
him out, too. To his credit, he was more relaxed now than
when I first met him. But, given his usual state of

constant tension, that didn't say much. Not that it mattered to me—I loved him just the way he was, jumpiness and all.

"*Some bacon and eggs will make us feel better,*" he said through our telepathic connection.

"They always do," I replied. "Almost like there's magic to it."

We took the long way toward the Outskirts. The day was already underway, and I wasn't looking to charge headfirst into a thick crowd when I was already feeling so emotionally spent. Eastwind was beautiful any day of the year, but on this particular mid-April day, when all the window boxes were overflowing with a full rainbow of flowers and the trees along the cobblestone streets were blooming fuchsia, it would have been a shame not to take a side street. I still passed a few familiar faces on my route, but they seemed to be serenely enjoying their walks as well, so we simply shared a quick wave as we passed one another. The small trickle of emotions I got from each of them was quite calming and peaceful anyway.

I didn't want to jinx myself, but I thought this might be a very good day ahead of me.

"Remind me to get something to go for Givens," I said as we reached the edge of town.

"*As if he doesn't get enough food as it is,*" Atlas replied. "*He's gonna get fat, and then what good will he be?*"

"Be nice," I said, nudging him on the shoulder with

my elbow. "Besides, commenting on someone else's diet is a bit rich, considering you're not only about to get a full breakfast platter but also whatever scraps you beg off the other tables with those big red puppy eyes."

"Not the same thing at all," Atlas replied. *"For one thing, I was underweight when I came out of the Deadwoods. I'm trying to bulk up. Don't you want a familiar who can protect you from all the danger you get yourself into? And also, Givens has a very clear job description. If he gets fat, you think he'll be able to do it with any sort of proficiency?"*

Too exhausted to counter his points, I sighed.

Givens was the studio cat at Time to Kiln. He'd come from rough beginnings, but now he had found his place and was thriving. In exchange for chasing any mice or critters out of the pottery studio, he got to live there, enjoy two massive meals a day (plus whatever treats people snuck him), and spend most of his daytime hours lounging in the perfect spot where the late afternoon sunbeams washed over him through the window.

He had once been a witch's familiar, though not to a kind witch, so he preferred to be nobody's familiar in particular, instead receiving care from the entire community of Time to Kiln students. I was the only one who could speak to him, using what was probably my favorite Fifth Wind power—one that I told almost no one about—the ability to communicate with familiars outside of my own. As far as anyone knew, I was the only witch in town with this power, and I was glad for it, because it meant

Givens had at least one person to talk to. Granted, most of his communication was complaints, but he'd earned that right.

There were Eastwinders who made a point of avoiding the Outskirts. Besides the diner, there wasn't much of a draw to this area unless you lived out here. It was wolf territory. The Scandrick compound was out here somewhere, though not within sight of Medium Rare, so I'd never actually seen it. Nora Ashcroft had once remarked that if I never had to go there, I could call my life a success. She had apparently had a few rough encounters with the Scandricks, who ran the compound along with other notorious families like the Saxons and the Hardys. I happened to know a few Saxons and Hardys—they ventured out more often.

Small clusters of run-down buildings dotted the area, but the most forbidding part of the Outskirts was how close it was to the Deadwoods. The Deadwoods had quite the reputation, and rightly so. Some of the most dangerous creatures in Eastwind could be found there. Werewolves, and occasionally werebears, roamed the woods to shift into their animal forms and cause trouble. The only reason I would ever willingly go back into the Deadwoods would be to visit Ted, whose cabin was tucked away out there. It goes without saying that a grim reaper was safe living among packs of hellhounds, hide-behinds, and countless other unnameable dangers.

When Medium Rare came into view, both Atlas and I paused to stare. I came to the diner at least twice a week, and I'd never seen anything like this before. The place was packed. Through the large windows, I could see that every table was full, and there was a large crowd gathered outside the front door, waiting for tables—easily two dozen people. And I didn't recognize a single one of them. What was going on?

Maybe it was the anxiety I was picking up from Atlas, but I nearly turned around and left. I'll admit, part of that was my own hesitation. I was already exhausted from last night's training, and the thought of walking through a crowd this thick made me even more tired. But I had told Nora I would come by.

"There's probably not a single open seat in there," I said, "so we can just pop in to let Nora know we're here and then leave. I'll get you a meat pie over at A New Leaf instead."

Atlas nodded his shaggy head, and I was surprised to find that when I started forward, he came with me. He really was getting braver. Or maybe he just didn't want to be left alone this close to the Deadwoods.

It was as overwhelming as I thought it would be, cutting through the group. Anticipation, anxiety, disgust, jealousy, guilt—and was that a touch of schadenfreude? There was a much more nuanced emotion that I was just beginning to sense. Maybe my training was working.

It didn't get much better once I was inside the diner. When I was living in New Orleans, I was accustomed to things being loud—parties on the street, loud gatherings in the apartment—and it really hadn't bothered me. It felt like life happening everywhere, and I simply got to soak it in. But since I'd come to Eastwind, my baseline for sound had gone way down. The noisiness of the diner felt almost like too much, even though much of the sound was friendly conversation and laughter. Perhaps if I wasn't feeling so encroached upon by the emotions, the noise wouldn't have bothered me.

Atlas was pressed against my side, possibly out of fear, but more likely because there wasn't much space left once we stepped inside. I looked around for Nora but didn't see her. She was probably back in the kitchen. A man sitting at the countertop turned, spotted me, and waved me over. It was Deputy Stu Manchester, who came into Medium Rare every morning after his shift to get a slice of cherry pie and a cup of coffee. Or, at least, it used to be after his shift, but now that he had Tanner Culpepper helping him with law enforcement around town, his seniority had allowed him to work days rather than nights, so he often came in right before his shift began.

Either way, he was in almost every day. Old habits died hard in Eastwind. As I approached him, I realized that the stool next to him was available. Once I was close enough, he pointed at it and said, "Miss Ashcroft was saving this for you. Wanted me to protect it with my life."

Dang. My plan to pop in and out had been foiled by the lionhearted deputy. Always protecting and serving, that one.

"Thanks," I said as I slid onto the stool and watched Atlas disappear behind the countertop, where Grim would no doubt be waiting.

I leaned toward Deputy Manchester so he could hear me and asked, "What's going on here?"

"Same thing that's going on everywhere lately: tourism."

"Tourism? From where?"

"Avalon mostly, as far as I'm aware," he said, turning a watchful eye over the crowd as he sipped from his coffee mug.

"Does this happen every year?" I asked. It was, after all, a beautiful time in Eastwind. Maybe this was just tourist season.

"We have tourists here from time to time, and they do like to come around this time of year. It's beautiful out. But it's never been like this. This is something new. I don't particularly care for it."

"Neither do I," said a voice from the other side of the counter. It was Nora, staring past me at the packed tables. A chunk of hair had fallen out of her ponytail, but she didn't seem to notice. There was a deep crease between her brows, and the corners of her mouth were slightly turned down. Looked like someone had had a rough morning.

"If I had the power to command ghosts to haunt someone, I would absolutely use that against Lot Flufferbum," she said.

"You mean all of this is from that article he wrote?" I

asked. Nora had told me a couple of months back that he was working on some sort of list of the top restaurants in Eastwind, but I hadn't heard much about it after she initially mentioned it. Last I'd heard, he was using the threat of it to try to get free food around town and to make a nuisance of himself as a customer.

Nora nodded. "Apparently Avalon's top newspaper picked it up. We're the hot spring vacation destination now." She rolled her eyes. "I've encountered my fair share of curses since being here, but this has gotta be the worst one yet."

I looked around at the crowd and noticed that the corner booth, which was usually reserved for Ted at this hour, was occupied by three high-fashion twenty-some-things (although, to be fair, they were elves, so they could've been over a hundred years old, and I wouldn't have known).

"Did Ted already leave?" I asked.

Nora shook her head. "He hasn't been in yet this morning."

"Hope that's not a bad omen," said Deputy Manchester.

"Most people think it's a good omen when Ted's a no-show," Nora replied.

Deputy Manchester rubbed his thumb and finger down his mustache. "Most people don't work with the reaper like I do. If he's not here, he may be headed to a murder that I'll be spending my whole shift dealing with and the next who-knows-how-long investigating."

"Maybe he just slept in," I suggested. Nora and the deputy made it clear what they thought about that naïve suggestion with their looks.

"Maybe one of his phoenixes caught something on fire," Nora suggested. "I wish I had the time to think about it more."

"It looks like you have some new help," I said, trying to lift her mood as I gestured toward a young man in an apron whom I didn't recognize.

"Jaymes Hardy. He's a good kid. A little... Well, he's fine. Here, I'll introduce you."

Nora waved at him once he was done taking a table's order, and he scurried over.

Since this was the first time I'd ever seen him, I couldn't tell whether he looked at everyone with those wide and adoring eyes or if only Nora earned that look from him. He had curly black hair that sat in a mop on his head, and dark lashes above chocolate-brown eyes. While Nora had called him a kid, I suspected he was only a few years younger than me, perhaps in his mid-twenties. His last name tipped me off to the fact that he was a werewolf, possibly one who called the Scandrick compound home.

"You need me?" he asked.

"Jaymes, this is Dahlia. She's in here a lot, so I thought you ought to be on a first-name basis."

Jaymes turned to me as a look of comprehension bloomed on his face. "Dahlia Wildes? You're the other Fifth Wind, right?"

It was still so strange to see my reputation precede me, but I managed not to get too thrown off. "Yeah, that's me. Nice to meet you."

Jaymes looked like he was about to speak, but before he could, Bryant, one of the servers who'd worked at Medium Rare longer than even Nora had, appeared by Nora's side. He didn't look happy. "Table eight wants to speak with the manager. They ordered their steak and eggs medium rare and sunny-side up. But apparently, when I dropped it off, the steak was cooked medium rare and the eggs were—you guessed it—sunny-side up."

Nora looked confused. "Their order came out correct?"

"Yes, and that man in the ridiculous ruffled hat is quite upset about it. I don't think he knows what medium rare or sunny-side up mean."

Nora glanced over Bryant's shoulder. "Oh, it's the tour guide, isn't it?"

"I don't know who he is, but I've been up since three a.m., and if he speaks down to me again, like I don't know what a hellhound medium rare steak looks like after working here for nine years—"

Nora held up her hand. "Deep breath. He's a jerk, I know. He was in here yesterday and tried to tell me that he ordered hash browns when he definitely ordered bacon. Some people compensate for a lack of brains with an overexaggerated amount of certainty. I'll handle him." She sighed, set her face into a forced smile that likely fooled nobody, and marched over to table eight.

I watched her go and treated myself to a good look at the difficult customer. His ruffled hat did look ridiculous and out of place in the casual setting of the diner, with the backdrop of the Deadwoods through the windows. He was dressed in a lavender and teal robe that clashed noticeably with his cerulean hat.

He watched Nora approach with a smug look, and I felt for her. I never understood why some people liked to make themselves a problem, but it certainly happened. Being rude to the people who made your food just seemed ill-advised anyway, all common decency and politeness aside. Of course, I knew that everyone who worked at Medium Rare cared too much about what they did to tamper with someone's food, no matter how difficult that person was. Perhaps the tour guide could sense that about this place, and that was why he was expressing himself so freely.

Nora kept her cool as he began to gesture at his plate, but I felt myself get squirmy just watching the unnecessary rudeness, so I turned back to the counter.

"Can I take your order?"

I'd almost forgotten that Jaymes was still standing next to me.

"Oh, yeah, sure," I said. He was one of those people who had a high tolerance for standing near someone. I struggled to name the emotion that was coming from him, partially because of the sea of emotions I was surrounded by, and partially because it was a strange emotion. Almost not an emotion, actually. The closest I could come to naming it was to call it intrigue. I felt the desire to scoot my chair closer to Deputy Manchester to create a little more distance from Jaymes, but I didn't want to offend him or hurt his feelings, so I simply leaned back slightly as I delivered my usual order and, of course, added something for Atlas.

By the time my food had arrived and I'd finished it off, the deputy was on his third coffee refill since I'd gotten there, and Ted still hadn't arrived. While the rude tour guide and his group had paid their bill and left, the diner was still packed. I ordered some cured salmon to go for Givens, bade Deputy Manchester goodbye, and headed for the door.

Just as Atlas stepped outside with me, a dark figure emerged in front of us.

"Good morning, Dahlia," said Ted. From behind the bottoms of his black robe, a ghost cat pounced into view.

"Everything okay?" I asked.

"Yeah, things are great! Why do you ask?"

"You're here a little later than usual," I said. "I thought maybe someone had... Maybe you were working."

"Oh! Yeah, I could see why you would think that. But I was just out at my cabin with Grace, Landon, and Monty. Monty is starting to shift into a wolf more frequently, so they thought it might be a smart idea to introduce him to the Deadwoods early. He won't be going there by himself for a long time, but you know how teenagers are. If he ever sneaks off, I'll be sure to keep an eye on him while he's in there."

"That's incredibly kind of you to keep an eye on him like that, Ted," I said.

He shrugged bashfully. "What can I say? I have a soft spot for that little kid."

"Well, I'd better get this back to Givens before he thinks I forgot about him."

Ted waved goodbye and made his way into Medium Rare. Out of curiosity, which had really been getting the better of me these days, I watched through the window as Ted approached his usual corner booth. I couldn't hear what he was saying to the three elves sitting in his spot, but I was sure it was something. Nonetheless, one glimpse at the grim reaper, and the three friends threw some coins on the table and quickly vacated the spot.

I felt an immediate hit of comfort at seeing something in Eastwind return to the way it was before the tourists.

I shook off the heavy layer of other people's emotions that still clung to my skin, and then Atlas and I made our way toward the studio to give Givens his late morning treat.

How long this tourist boom would last, I couldn't begin to guess. But at least Ted was settled into his spot in the corner booth, which meant that nobody had died.

Yet.

But that would change before the day's end.

Chapter Two

❧

Atlas opted to stay home on my casual date night with Dante. My boyfriend—it still made me giddy to call him that after two months of it being official—was meeting me down at Sheehan's Pub after his shift finished at Franco's Pizza.

The days were getting longer, but it was almost completely dark by the time I reached the main street leading down to the pub. I didn't mind walking alone at night in Eastwind. Maybe I should have been more cautious, but I genuinely felt safe in this town, even without Atlas.

Most of the other townsfolk had already gone home for the evening and were settling down with a cup of tea or a book, allowing me to walk large portions of my route to Sheehan's without seeing a single other person.

The world around me was silent, but not as silent as the wings of the owl that swooped out of the sky and landed on a bench ahead of me. He looked at me directly, squawking, and then held out one of his feet. A small slip of rolled-up paper—a message. I accepted the offering, taking it gently so as not to upset one of the owls and get on bad terms with the entire mail system of Eastwind, and then I unrolled the slip and read the message inside. It was from Dante.

Slammed at work. Larger crowd than expected. Won't be cut early. Probably not finished until after midnight. So sorry. Already told Jane she owes me a day off to make it up to you.

  —Dante

That was certainly a bummer, but I could tell that he was just as upset about it as I was, possibly more so because it meant he had to work late. Meanwhile, I was just enjoying my day off.

It sounded like Franco's Pizza might have made the top restaurants list too. I giggled nervously to myself when I thought about how Jane might be handling the neediness of tourists slightly less diplomatically than Nora did. I was sure Dante would have stories to share the next time I saw him.

Since I was already nearly to the pub, I decided to pop in anyway and see who might be there.

But when Sheehan's came into view, I found myself

reconsidering my plan. As with Medium Rare that morning, it had a crowd spilling out of the front doors. I didn't recognize any of the people, either.

"Oh boy," came a voice from behind me. I turned and saw Grace and Landon walking up together, holding hands.

It had been Landon who spoke, and Grace nudged him with her shoulder. "We're not backing out now. Not when we have a sitter for Monty. And maybe it's a little different of a date night than we had planned, but maybe something interesting will happen." She waved to me as they approached.

"You and Dante had a date night planned too?"

"We did, but he's being held up at work, so I thought I'd just come and say hello to whoever was here. I didn't know there would be so many people to say hello to. And a lot of people I would have to introduce myself to before I even said hello."

Grace, always observant, was able to read between the lines.

"No, no, you're not going home," she said, grabbing my hand and practically dragging both Landon and me behind her.

"She didn't used to be like this, you know," Landon said to me. "She used to be a homebody who would just sit around and read books while I left the house and came to the pub."

"What can I say?" Grace replied. "Motherhood has made me less of a homebody."

The inside of Sheehan's Pub felt louder than it actually was due to the high volume of emotions around me. They created a palpable cacophony all on their own. It was tricky enough for me to be in a crowd to begin with, but pack a bunch of people indoors, and it was like the emotions had nowhere to vent. At least outdoors they seemed to dissipate slightly in the open air, but in here they had little place to go, echoing off the walls. Add in the fact that alcohol consumption had a tendency to heighten and intensify emotions, and I felt nearly drunk without having had a single sip of alcohol myself.

We paused inside and looked around for an open table. The odds seemed heavily stacked against us finding anywhere to sit, but we lucked out when Landon spotted a group getting up from a corner booth only a few seconds after we began searching. He rushed over and slid in, their finished tankards still sweating onto the table in front of him. Grace and I caught up to him.

"And it's a corner booth, too," he said. "That's better for your... powers, right?"

I nodded. I'd heard Landon described before as socially awkward, but the predominant quality I'd attribute to him was consideration. He didn't necessarily understand what my powers were—to be fair, no one did yet—but he knew a few facts about them. One of them was that it was easier for me to be on the periphery of a group rather than right in the middle of it. The corner booth also provided some shelter from the ruckus of the place. We might actually be able to enjoy a conversation without having to yell "what?" every five seconds.

Grace gathered up the empties from the table and wove her way through the crowd to drop them off for Fiona at the bar.

"Who are all these people?" Landon asked. Before I could answer, he added, "Obviously, they're tourists because I definitely don't recognize them from here. So perhaps the better question is, why all the tourists?"

I explained to him about Flufferbum's article.

"And Sheehan's Pub made the list?" He didn't hide his incredulity.

"I don't know. I haven't seen the full list yet. I suppose they do serve food here," I replied.

"Sure, but it's the kind of food that only tastes good after your third beer."

"Maybe Flufferbum had three beers before he ate."

My gaze landed on a group of people I recognized from the diner that morning. Sure enough, the fussy tour guide in his cerulean hat was positioned in the middle of them. As he spoke, everyone in the group offered him an avid audience. He threw his hands into the air, mimicking some sort of explosion, and his audience laughed on cue.

Grace returned a moment later with three tankards of cold beer, setting them down in front of us. She was wide-eyed as she plopped onto the bench next to me. "Quite a lot going on," she said.

"If you're overwhelmed," Landon said, "we can still go home."

"Absolutely not," she said. "Each person here is a system of moving parts. Emotions, thoughts, histories, hopes, and dreams. With this many people packed in together, you know something interesting is going to happen. Statistically, it's almost guaranteed. I don't want to miss that."

While I understood her sentiment, I wasn't sure I felt the same way. She was right that this was essentially a powder keg, especially as the night wore on and people got further intoxicated. Something would likely go down. But did I want to be here for that? Not particularly.

I knew Grace enjoyed being a fly on the wall for that sort of thing, getting to observe it from a distance and deconstruct all the different human factors that had led up to it. I, on the other hand, had spent most of my life being a fly on the wall in my old life in New Orleans, and while it had allowed me to observe human behavior from a mostly safe distance, things had changed since then.

In Eastwind, I was one of only three Fifth Wind witches, which meant that if the drama got serious enough, I would likely have to get involved whether I wanted to or not. But also, I had developed these gosh-darn powers that kept me from being able to maintain emotional distance and simply observe things. Unfortunately, that meant that witnessing drama had much less of a draw for me now. Not to mention, I had never been a huge fan of conflict, even if the conflict was someone else's. It always made me want to leave a room.

"Uh," said Landon. "This can't be good."

I followed his line of sight and saw that an elf had just entered the pub. The door hadn't fully closed behind her before she was halfway across the room toward the bar. She was angry, that was clear enough to see on her face. Her eyes were locked in on... something.

"Who is that?" I asked.

"Naomi Twench," Landon replied. "She's married to—"

"Delphelius Twench!" the angry elf shouted, her voice carrying above the din. "You useless pile of refuse!"

The pub fell silent. She no longer needed to yell to be heard, but she yelled all the same as she got up in the face of one of the regulars I'd seen here frequently but had never spoken to. Apparently, he was named Delphelius, and he had done something to gravely upset his wife.

Delphelius was seated at the bar, with a large tankard cradled between his palms. He didn't look up as she continued to yell.

"You promised me!" she said. "You promised me that this time it would be different, that you would finally tackle the known problem in our back garden and stop wasting your life away in this cursed pub. Look at you! Sitting here by yourself in a room full of people. You don't even come here to spend time with friends. Just wasting your life away, as always. This is what I get for believing your promises. You've been useless since the moment we married. Forced me into settling down with you, and then never lifted a finger to help again. You're as useful to me alive as you would be dead, you miserable old witch! I hope you enjoy that drink of yours fully, because when you come home, I won't be there. This time I mean it. I've had enough. And unlike you, I follow through with my promises. Don't come looking for me, though I'm sure that would be more effort than you would ever consider putting into our relationship!"

She turned her laser-sharp gaze on Fiona behind the bar. "Sorry to tell you this, but you're about to lose one of your most loyal customers. He's been buying those drinks with my family's money for decades now. But I'm done." She looked around and seemed to realize for the first time that the place was packed and all eyes were on her. "Looks like you're not hurting for business anyway." She leaned back over her husband and added, "See? They won't miss you here when you die. You could have built something with me, but you didn't. And now it's too late. Nobody's gonna miss you when you die, you no-good heap of soiled robes."

As clear as her rage felt to me, something else cut through it briefly like a knife, an emotion I didn't expect given the situation: glee. Was that coming from Naomi? What would she feel so gleeful about? The thought of his death?

She turned quickly on her heel and, without another glance at her audience, stomped right back out of the pub. The door closed slowly behind her, and while the conversations slowly resumed, Delphelius Twench remained exactly where he was at the bar, the tankard still cradled between his palms. Had he even heard her? Did he care?

A shudder ran down my spine as I tried to rid myself of Naomi's stifling rage that had snuck inside me while watching that interaction. The woman was not messing around. I didn't know anything about her, but I knew she meant what she had just said. Meanwhile, I hadn't gotten much from Delphelius throughout that interaction, unless, of course, the glee was his, which seemed unlikely. He didn't appear moved by the public scolding at all, which was strange. How could a married couple get to the point where one of them cared so deeply and the other cared so little? And how many fights like this had they had before?

"See?" said Grace. "I told you something interesting would happen."

Landon's cheeks were flushed, his eyes wide. "If I ever make you want to do that to me, Grace, I give you permission to just go ahead and put a pillow over my face first. I don't think I could survive that kind of humiliation anyway."

"It doesn't seem to have affected him much," I said. "If he moved an inch, I didn't see it."

"I wouldn't have married you if I thought it would ever get to that," Grace said. "But sure, I love you enough to put a pillow over your face when you're sleeping rather than shout at you in public."

I couldn't help but laugh. "Sounds like true love."

Grace and I got to talking about our works in progress at the pottery studio. She had been carving luminaries that she planned on selling ahead of the Day of the Dead in the fall. They were beautiful creations with intricate carving. I had seen her prototype with a candle beneath it, and the light had practically danced over every wall of the room. It had made the space feel like a purified sanctuary. I planned on buying one from her. They were exquisite. Meanwhile, after half a year of practice, I was working on... mugs. To give myself credit, I was getting better at the bodies. The handles, on the other hand, were giving me quite a bit of trouble.

As she was describing her plans to carve one of the luminaries with small animal shapes so that she could put it in Monty's bedroom to help him fall asleep, I looked over and noticed that Delphelius Twench was no longer in his spot at the bar. Had the public scolding actually compelled him to chase after his wife? Would he apologize? It hadn't felt like she'd gotten through to him at all, but perhaps he was just good at hiding it.

Oliver Bridgewater and Zoe Clementine were high-fiving after presumably beating a pair of tourists at a game of scufflepuck when the pub door opened again, and in walked Jaymes Hardy.

I must have seen him before meeting him that morning at Medium Rare, but as mean as it sounds, he was the kind of person who was easily forgotten. He wasn't unattractive, but he also wasn't attractive. He had average features and moved about in a way that reminded me of a slinking dog, hoping that going unnoticed might allow him to maintain some of his freedom to move about. I wondered if he had learned the hard way that the easiest way of being a werewolf around town was to be an inconspicuous werewolf around town. Of all the families that lived out at the Scandrick compound, the Hardys seemed to be some of the most liked. There were a lot of them, though, so I was sure a few had gotten into trouble before. Had Jaymes been one of those?

He scanned the crowd, presumably looking for friends he was meeting here, but his gaze skipped over everyone until it landed on me. We locked eyes. He smiled, waved, and headed my way.

Was he here to see me? Maybe Nora had wanted someone to deliver a message for her. She could have just sent an owl, though...

Jaymes paused at the edge of our table. "Hey, Dahlia!"

Grace and Landon shared a quick glance across me.

"Hi, Jaymes," I said. "Do you know Grace and Landon?"

"I've seen them around here," he said. "Hi, I'm Jaymes Hardy."

Grace squinted at him. "Oh, wait, I do remember you. But you were a teenager then. I think I saw you at the Scandrick compound once."

Jaymes looked surprised. "You were at the Scandrick compound? But aren't you a witch?"

"A North Wind," she replied. "Yes, but I... had a friend there that I knew."

Landon quickly leaned across both of us to offer his hand to Jaymes. "Landon Hawker. Nice to meet you. I'm Grace's husband."

They shook hands, and quickly Jaymes's attention returned to me. "I'm so glad we finally got to meet today. It's so crazy that there are three Fifth Wind witches in Eastwind now, huh?"

I had only ever known Eastwind to have three Fifth Wind witches, but to be polite, I said, "Yeah, I guess that is pretty unusual."

"Do you do a lot of necromancy?" he asked.

"Huh?"

"A lot of necromancy," he repeated. "That's what Fifth Wind witches do, right?"

I glanced at Grace, who seemed to be as curious about this conversation as I was. "Yes, I guess that is technically what I do. I like to think of it more as spirit magic. But necromancy isn't technically incorrect."

"So you can speak to ghosts and stuff?"

"Yes," I said. "Whether or not they feel like talking to me is a different story."

Jaymes certainly had an interesting fascination with my powers. I decided to chalk it up to something guys his age might naturally be interested in. Goodness knew there were enough men in their early twenties dabbling in necromancy back in New Orleans, and we didn't even have Fifth Winds there.

"Have you ever brought anything back from the dead?" he asked. I opened my mouth to respond, but before I could, something quite unexpected happened.

Delphelius Twench appeared right by our table, next to Jaymes. As a ghost.

"You're the Fifth Wind," he said, "so you can see me."

I nodded.

"Good. I need you to follow me. Pretty sure I was just murdered."

Chapter Three

I looked at Grace, Landon, and Jaymes and said, "Would you excuse me for just one second? I'll be right back."

Grace slid out of the booth so I could get out as well, and as calmly as I could, I followed Delphelius's ghost toward the exit of the pub. He disappeared straight through the front door, and just as I reached to open it, the door swung open, nearly hitting me in the face. I jumped back.

"I'm so terribly sorry!" It was the tour guide in his frilly blue hat. He blinked at me. "Oh," he said. "You are the Fifth Wind witch, aren't you?"

I didn't like the greediness in his tone. He was looking at me like he might collect me to put in a display case somewhere. I was glad to have somewhere else to be, even though the circumstances were rather morbid.

"Yes, that's me," I said quickly, and then squeezed past him out the door. The small patio out front was packed, but I was able to walk around the perimeter of it to follow Delphelius's ghost. One of the tourists was bracing himself against a lamppost by the street, aggressively emptying the contents of his stomach. Boy, things were really getting out of hand.

Delphelius turned the corner around the edge of the building into a small side alleyway. As soon as I turned the corner myself, I saw it. The body.

In every meaningful way, I'd known this was what I would find. After all, I was following the man's ghost. That could really only mean one thing. And yet it was still a shock to my system to see the person who had just been alive, albeit mostly unresponsive, sitting at the bar, now lying facedown with his arms and legs spread, in a dark alley.

"There I am," said the spirit impassively. One might think a ghost would be a little more upset about being murdered, but I was starting to get the feeling that Delphelius was mostly a stranger to emotion.

"Yes," I said. "There you are. Dead."

The ghost shrugged. "Just thought someone ought to know." And then he disappeared, leaving me alone in a side alley next to a pub with a freshly dead body.

It occurred to me that if anyone were to walk around and see me, I would look very suspicious. That thought helped snap me out of my stupor, and I scurried back around to the front of the building, rang the bell so that an owl appeared, and then sent an emergency message straight to the sheriff's department. It read:

> Delphelius Twench is dead. Not sure
> how. His ghost came and found me and
> led me to the side of Sheehan's Pub.
> Please come quickly. -Dahlia

I sent it off, and then I stood at the corner of the building, trying to act nonchalant, as if there wasn't a dead body only a few yards away from me. I waited for Stu, Tanner, or Sheriff Bloom—whoever was available—to come clean up this mess, as the drunken tourist continued to brace himself against the lamppost and relieve himself of all the food he had enjoyed throughout the day from Eastwind's top restaurants.

* * *

"You said Delphelius Twench came and got you?" asked Deputy Manchester. We stood out front of Sheehan's, out of view of the alley where the body remained until Ted finished loading it into his new body conveyance to take it down to the sheriff's department. Until the magical examiner and medical examiner could each inspect the body of Delphelius Twench, we wouldn't know how he died. Unless, of course, Delphelius himself gave us a heads-up. Unfortunately, he hadn't dropped back in after disappearing.

"He did," I confirmed. "He wanted to show me that he was dead."

"And did he, you know, happen to mention what happened?" asked the deputy.

"No. He just said he thought he'd been murdered."

Deputy Manchester's thick eyebrows rose toward his hairline. "He said that? He thought it was murder?"

I nodded.

"Did he clarify why he believed that?"

"He didn't," I replied. "He didn't clarify much before he disappeared."

Deputy Manchester scanned the surroundings vaguely. "Disappeared, eh? Already? Could you bring him back?"

I cringed apologetically. "I don't know how to."

"It would help to have a word with him."

"Maybe he'll turn up again."

Or maybe he doesn't have any unfinished business to keep him around. I didn't say that to Deputy Manchester, because I didn't think it would alleviate his concerns about figuring out what had happened here. Maybe the only unfinished business Delphelius had to keep tethered to this plane was simply to have someone find his body. Maybe he didn't care who murdered him. He certainly didn't strike me as a man too attached to living.

Deputy Manchester ran this thumb and pointer down his mustache, and I could feel the anxiety radiating from him. "As long as there's a possibility that it's homicide and we have no idea who might be behind it, I don't suppose it would be wise to leave the portal open to Avalon."

"You think it might've been one of the tourists?" I asked.

"Could be a tourist, sure. But if an Eastwinder did this, they might try to go on the lam, too. I don't like risking it. Not when we aren't working from a single suspect or even a person of interest yet."

"Well," I said, wondering if I should even mention it. I hated to create suspicion around anyone, especially a newly widowed woman, but someone would say something eventually if I didn't. "You might want to talk to Naomi Twench."

"Naomi? Delphelius's wife?"

"Yeah. She came by the pub earlier and had a lot to say to him."

"And what *specifically* makes you think I ought to talk to her?"

She'd said quite a lot in a short amount of time, and my attention had naturally flowed more toward her emotions than the words themselves, but a few phrases had lodged themselves in my memory. "She told him, 'You're as useful to me alive as you would be dead.' I don't know whether she really meant it or if she was speaking from a place of hurt and anger, like plenty of people do."

He nodded. "We don't need to know that yet. You're right, it sounds like I should speak with her about it, either way. If for nothing else than to rule her out so we don't waste time trying to prove something that isn't true."

Tanner, who had just started his shift on duty as Deputy Manchester's was wrapping up, had cast a magical barrier at the entrance to the side alley and was now interviewing folks who had been enjoying themselves out on the patio around the time of Delphelius's death. Most of them were tourists, and they appeared excited, not just as one might with the adrenaline of being so close to a possible killing as it took place, but rather as someone might when they were already rehearsing how they'd tell this story to their friends the following day.

It felt ungenerous of me to see it that way, but I struggled to see it any other way with how they conducted themselves. Delphelius's death was more of a tourist attraction than the loss of a life to them.

A yawn broke free from me, and Deputy Manchester grunted. "I couldn't agree more. I'm gonna let Deputy Culpepper take it from here. If you can give me fifteen minutes, I'll walk you home."

"Oh, you don't have to do that," I said.

"Legally? No. But morally? Yes, Miss Wildes, I do. I couldn't let you walk home alone without your familiar when there might be a killer on the loose and you were the one who discovered the body."

"You don't think I did it, then?" I asked.

The deputy's brows pinched together. "You know, the thought hadn't occurred to me. Maybe I'm losing my edge in this line of work."

I waved him off. "Forget I said it."

"Did you do this?" he asked.

"Unfortunately, no."

"Unfortunately?" He narrowed his eyes at me.

"Yes, because if I did it and could confess, you'd have this whole thing wrapped up."

He chuckled. "Fair point. I'd be shocked, though. You'd be the first Fifth Wind I've met who'd want to add one more ghost to their lives. Usually, you folks are doing everything you can to get rid of them."

* * *

I decided to take Deputy Manchester up on his offer to chaperone me home, more to ease his mind than because I thought I'd need the protection, and as I let myself inside Nora and Tanner's house and creeped into my bedroom to keep from possibly waking up any of the familiars, I found Atlas sitting by the bedroom window, waiting for me.

A moonbeam through the curtains illuminated his shaggy white face, which he had pointed my direction when I entered. *"What trouble were you causing?"* he asked.

"Huh?"

"You had a deputy escorting you."

I laughed. "I wasn't being detained. He was protecting me."

Atlas pressed his ears back flat against his head. *"From what?"*

It was late, and I didn't want to freak Atlas out, but honesty still felt like the best option. "Someone was found dead outside of Sheehan's Pub tonight."

Atlas didn't move a muscle as he stared at me. *"Bopped to death?"* he asked.

"No. I don't think so. I didn't get a good look at him, but it didn't look like a bopping. Hopefully, the medical examiner will know more about that soon."

He seemed to relax. *"As long as there's not a serial bopper out there and you've locked the doors behind you, then I suppose we'll be okay."*

While I didn't quite follow his logic—after all, being bopped on the head wasn't the only way people were murdered in Eastwind—I didn't want to get him worked up. "I locked all the doors behind me. We'll be safe from boppers tonight."

He leapt onto the bed and settled himself at the foot of it. *"Then I guess I can finally go to sleep."* I didn't miss the judgment in his statement. He didn't approve of me staying out so late. I suspected it was less about propriety and more about the fact that he struggled to go to sleep without knowing I was next to him.

I yawned. "Let me just brush my teeth and then—"

I yelped and jumped back when the spirit of Delphelius Twench appeared between me and my bathroom door. My heart raced, and it put a little bit of boldness in me. "Excuse me," I said, blinking. "You can't just barge into my bedroom like that."

I glanced at the bed. Atlas had already vacated his

spot, and I could see the top of his back poking out of his hiding spot on the other side of the bed.

Delphelius said nothing, and certainly didn't apologize. "You scared my familiar," I added.

He shrugged. "I need your help still, I guess."

"About your murder?"

He nodded, and I waited for him to continue. He didn't.

"What about it?" I demanded. I should've just told him to leave me alone until the morning and definitely not drop into my room again, but I had the feeling that he was the fickle and unreliable type, and if I wanted information from him that might help out Deputy Manchester, I would need to take it whenever it was offered and not be picky.

Still, I couldn't stop feeling annoyed with him.

"I think somebody killed me," he said.

This was like pulling teeth. I refrained from a sarcastic "No kidding" and went instead with, "Did you see anyone right before you died?"

He shook his head and offered little more.

I sighed, grabbed a throw blanket off the chair in the corner, and wrapped it around my shoulders before sitting down on my bed, legs crossed. Might as well be comfortable if this was going to take all night. "Can you tell me about what happened in the moments leading up to your death? Do you remember walking into the alley at all?"

"Yep. I was sitting at the bar. Fiona said she would

pour me another, but she was taking her sweet time about it. I had to relieve myself, so I told the couple next to me to watch my seat. Didn't want any tourists taking it. Went to the restroom, but it was full. Only had to take a leak, so I figured the weather was nice enough to go outside."

I wrinkled my nose. "You went into the alley to pee?"

"Might as well. Better than waiting."

Couldn't say I agreed with him, but showing my disapproval was likely a fast way for him to shut down completely. "So, you walk outside into the alley. Did you notice anyone following you? See anything suspicious?"

"Wasn't paying attention. Just had to take a leak."

"No one said anything to you? No 'Hey, Delphelius!' Nothing?"

With a shrug, he said, "Nah."

I gripped the throw blanket tighter so I wouldn't accidentally reach out and try to shake him by the shoulders. It wouldn't have worked, and it likely would've ruined whatever rapport I was beginning to build with him. If any.

"How about who might've wanted you dead?" I asked. "Your wife was pretty mad at you this evening."

"She's always mad at me." He didn't appear bothered by the fact.

"Do you think she might've finally had enough?"

"She's all bark and no bite, but who knows? She seemed sick of me, didn't she?"

I was starting to understand some of her animosity.

She'd called him useless, and if *this* interaction were any indicator...

"Anyone else?" I asked. "You have other enemies in Eastwind?"

"Probably."

I waited for more. When it was clear none was coming, I said, "Who might those people be?"

"Dunno. I seem to rub a lot of people the wrong way."

"You don't say."

How this man could manage to be so uninterested in his own murder was beyond me. It seemed like if he would be passionate about a single thing in his life, it ought to be finding who killed him. After all, if he truly didn't care, why was he still around? Nora said that plenty of people died and their spirits moved on with Ted right away. Only the ones with unfinished business stuck around.

If Delphelius had unfinished business, it seemed likely due to the fact that he'd never started the business in the first place. He didn't seem to have an ounce of motivation in his body, other than the motivation to sit at Sheehan's all day and drink.

Could that be it? Could he be tethered to this realm rather than moving on because he wanted to spend more time at Sheehan's?

I inhaled deeply, letting it out slowly to try to steady myself. "Let me get this straight," I said. "You want me to help you figure out who murdered you, correct?"

"Eh," he replied. "I guess so."

"And you were, presumably, *present* at your death."

"Seems like it."

"And you have zero information to help narrow down who might've done it."

"That's right."

I stared at him, hoping he would figure out my next question without me having to say it.

He did not.

"Then my next question," I continued, "is why are you still in my bedroom?"

He looked around and seemed to realize where he was for the first time. "Huh." And then he disappeared.

Chapter Four

Since I'd had quite the day off work the day before, I was more than happy to be behind the desk at the Time to Kiln pottery shop. It was a slow morning, which allowed me time to send an owl to Stu Manchester, letting him know that Delphelius had visited me the night before and offered a whole plate of nothing useful about his death.

I was hoping that would be that, and maybe I could leave this rest of the investigation up to the professionals, but I soon learned that that had been wishful thinking.

The owl arrived around ten in the morning, carrying the message from Deputy Manchester:

> Miss Wildes,
> We would be endlessly grateful for your presence at the sheriff's department at your

earliest convenience. We've run into a hitch in the Twench case that only your powers are suited to.

Best regards,
Deputy Manchester

I read the letter twice. It was strange to think that there was a single thing I could do that trained professionals like Deputy Manchester, Tanner, and even Sheriff Bloom couldn't manage. Manchester was a were-elk, which meant that if the magic required didn't involve shifting, he was probably out of luck. Tanner was a West Wind witch, or a Terramancer, which meant he was good with earth- and plant-based magic. And Gabby Bloom was an angel, which meant... I wasn't sure what she could do, but I understood it to be a lot. She was probably the only person in Eastwind who knew all she could do. Ruby True, her longtime friend, probably didn't even know it all.

And yet they needed my powers. So, so strange to consider.

I peeked into the studio, where Raven was demonstrating tall cylinders on the wheel for a class of eight students. When she completed the pull she was on, I tapped her on the shoulder. She smiled up at me from her stool, her hands muddy with slip. "Yes?"

"Deputy Manchester asked me to go down to the

sheriff's department when I have a moment. Could I take off a half-hour early today?"

Raven's eyes widened. "Is this about...?"

Word sure did travel fast in town.

I nodded.

"Forget about leaving a half-hour early. Just flip the sign to closed and go now."

"Are you sure?"

"Absolutely. And maybe come back afterward and update me on the investigation."

Ah yes. There was always a catch, huh? I could leave early if I paid with good gossip. This studio produced a lot of interesting work, but the thing it produced the most of, I'd learned, was a proliferation of gossip.

I bit back a smile. "I'll tell you as much as I can."

"Fair enough!" She returned to her cylinder.

Atlas left the shop by my side, and the two of us set out for the sheriff's department.

I hadn't been in the actual offices yet, and I found myself a little nervous about it. The imposing building didn't help. It was a rectangular brick structure, all sharp corners and no nonsense. When I got to the glass doors, I wondered if I ought to knock. But then I saw that the reception desk was through a long lobby, and I didn't want to make the receptionist get up, so I held open the door for Atlas and let myself in.

It was a quiet space, which surprised me. Maybe there wasn't a lot going on in Eastwind as far as crime, but I'd expected it to be a space of conflict and protestation. Instead, it was quiet. So quiet that I could hear the scratching of pen on parchment from the receptionist's desk.

I hadn't encountered many goblins in Eastwind, but when the receptionist finally bothered to look up at us, I saw that I was dealing with one now. They were short and pudgy creatures, and the stereotype was that they were short tempered. I didn't much buy into stereotypes as a practice, though. People had all kinds of stereotypes about Fifth Winds that I didn't fall into, and if that was true for me, that was probably true for others.

"Heaven forbid," the goblin said as his eyes landed on Atlas. "I *know* that's not another hellhound walking into these offices."

Atlas froze.

"What?" I asked.

"If he pees on my desk, I'll have you arrested."

Not quite the greeting I was expecting, having been asked to show up there. "What?"

"The big black one. Bladder bigger than his body. I couldn't get the smell out no matter how much I scrubbed. Ended up having to get a brand-new desk."

"Grim?" I said. "He marked your desk?"

"Marked? More like scarred it for life."

"Oh. Um. Atlas won't do that. He's potty trained." I knew as soon as I said it that Atlas would bristle at the description, which made him sound like some sort of pet rather than the autonomous beast that he was. And sure enough, he muttered something quietly to me about it. I ignored it.

"The black one was, too. Made no difference."

"Was that, um, recently?"

Another voice joined the conversation. "That was years ago, Jingo. Time to let it go." Deputy Manchester appeared in the lobby, next to the front desk. "This way, Miss Wildes. And Atlas is more than welcome in here." He shot Jingo a stern look, but the goblin just rolled his eyes and went back to writing notes.

The deputy showed us into a side room that turned out to be a small office. The space was made to feel much smaller by the stacks of filing boxes lining the walls. "I appreciate you coming so quickly, Miss Wildes," he said. "I hope it didn't interfere with your job."

"Raven didn't mind me leaving, but she will want to have a scoop about why you brought me in."

Deputy Manchester sighed. It didn't look to me like he'd managed to get more than a couple of hours' sleep after walking me home the night before. "That's how it works in town, certainly. I'll ask that you exercise discretion about what you share with her and others, though, for the integrity of the investigation."

"Of course," I said.

"That being said, it's entirely likely that you leave here with nothing to share at all. That's the problem: we have Naomi Twench in custody, but she's not talking. We were hoping you could step in there with her."

"Oh. I, uh, I don't know how to interview someone. Not like a deputy."

He waved me off. "We're not asking that. Like I said, I'm pretty sure she's not going to speak with us. And that presents a problem. I couldn't get any information out of her, so I brought in Sheriff Bloom to try. The sheriff has the power of Judgment, as an angel. She can tell if someone's lying to her. But it doesn't work if the person won't say anything, and Mrs. Twench is keeping her mouth tighter than a vampire's coffin on the summer solstice. But you don't need someone to talk to get a read on them, correct?"

Ah, it made sense why I was here now. "That's correct, for the most part. I'm still not very strong with controlling that, though. I can direct it a little bit, but sometimes—"

"Never fear, Miss Wildes. If you can't get a read on her, we're no worse than before. It's only a bonus if you can. I appreciate you even trying." He paused, took a deep breath that once again gave away his exhaustion—perhaps from more than just lack of sleep—then said, "Ready to see her?"

I looked down at Atlas.

"Need me to go with you?" he offered.

The only time I'd ever laid eyes on Naomi Twench was while she was publicly chewing out her now-deceased husband. Maybe she was kind and gentle normally, but I had no way of knowing that. *"If you don't mind,"* I replied.

Deputy Manchester led us down a hallway and through a locked door, on the other side of which ran two rows of holding cells. The ones on my right were barred, but the ones on the left were more like interview rooms I'd seen on TV, with a small square window looking in through a solid wood door. Naomi was in one of those.

Her eyes locked onto me when I stepped inside behind the deputy. I felt a chill run through me, but didn't sense any particular emotion. No hatred, anger, or even fear. That was a good sign, I supposed.

"Mrs. Twench, this is Dahlia Wildes. She's going to sit in with us for a few more questions."

Naomi continued to sit up straight in her chair, carrying herself with a certain obstinate dignity despite the circumstances. Whether she knew that I was a Fifth Wind was anybody's guess. I'd once overheard Nora and Tanner talking about a hidden village within Eastwind where many of the elves lived, so it was possible that she lived there, far away from the local gossip of the rest of us. She might not have known a new Fifth Wind had entered the realm half a year ago.

Or maybe she did. There was no telling what she did and didn't know, because I wasn't getting a single emotion off her yet.

She was seated on one side of the table, facing the door, and across from her were two wooden chairs. Deputy Manchester pulled one out for me, and I took a seat. He settled in on my left. "Mrs. Twench, I know I've asked you some of these questions before, so I hope you'll forgive me for asking them again now that Dahlia's here. If you have any questions for either of us, feel free to ask."

Naomi showed no recognition that he'd even spoken. She simply continued to stare a hole through me. I noted how strange it was that she didn't spare a thought for the large albino hellhound, who was arguably the most dangerous individual in the room with her.

"What was it in particular that set you off last night, Mrs. Twench?"

I waited, tried to tune in. Oh no, was I really this bad at the one thing I could do that nobody else could?

But then I caught it, like the end of a clear piece of fishing wire. Easy to overlook, but once I saw it, I locked in. It was the emotion behind her mask. She was certainly good at keeping it all hidden, better than anyone else I'd encountered, but now that I saw the thread, I could grasp it. And it felt like bitterness. I tugged on it, and out came something more: rage.

Naomi didn't speak a word, though, and her expression remained stony as she continued to stare at me.

I shot the deputy a look and nodded as discreetly as I could.

He continued asking the questions. "Is it true that you told your husband at Sheehan's Pub that he'd be as useful to you dead as he would be alive?"

I held on tight to that thread, and what it led me to was another emotion: betrayal. Naomi might be chock-full of emotions hidden far away. I tried not to get excited, as it could make me lose my focus. I imagined myself leaning in closer to her.

The deputy didn't wait for a response. He neither expected nor needed one. Instead, he continued to ask his questions.

"Did Delphelius ever hit you?"

Her rage ebbed until Deputy Manchester asked the next question: "Did you ever hit him?"

The rage resumed, more powerful than before. What did that mean? Did it mean she'd been physically violent with him? Did that point to her guilt in his murder?

"Do you know who is responsible for his death?" Deputy Manchester asked.

I sensed no change in her after that question. If there was guilt, she was hiding it from me. Or maybe she did know who was responsible—maybe it was her—and she simply felt no guilt.

"How was your marriage with Delphelius leading up to your altercation with him at Sheehan's last night?"

The tenacity of her rage lessened, and I felt something softer underneath. The closest I could come to it with my limited training so far was sadness. That was a broad category, though. Was she remorseful? Lonely? Despairing? I wished I was better at distinguishing.

"One last question, and then I'll tell Jingo to order you some lunch. Are you glad your husband is dead?"

Her expression finally shifted the slightest bit, and the tiniest hint of a smile poked at the corner of her lips. While she said nothing, I felt a conflicting emotion. At first, I thought it might be the glee that I'd felt wash through the pub as she chewed out her husband. It seemed natural to assume that emotion had belonged to her. But this wasn't quite that. While her changed expression hinted at something akin to joy, though no doubt a corrupted form of it, the emotion I sensed from her now was more aligned with disgust. But for what? That her husband was dead or that he'd lived for so long?

Deputy Manchester checked in with me, and while I didn't understand what all the emotions had meant, I'd made a mental note of which ones went with each question so that I could update him once we were able to leave this tiny holding room. I nodded to let him know I was good to go if he was.

He stood, and I made to follow, but before I could, Naomi reached across the table and grabbed my wrist. Deputy Manchester already had his back to us and missed it, but Atlas saw it and showed his teeth. The second her hand made contact with my skin, I felt a jolt of rage and wicked relief shoot through me.

Naomi leaned forward and finally broke her silence. "Please find out who did this to my husband. I want to thank them."

I yanked my wrist free but continued to stare at her for a moment longer.

"Miss Wildes?"

I blinked and quickly got up out of my seat, following the deputy back into the hallway.

* * *

"It's hard to connect a single emotion to a motivation for it," I explained to Deputy Manchester once we were back in the cramped office.

"But you got a read on some of her emotions?" He looked hopeful. I hated to be the one to disappoint him.

"I did." We walked through each of the questions he'd asked and what I'd sensed from her, and by the end of it, he had a deep crease between his brows and was stroking his mustache thoughtfully.

"Certainly something there, but you're right. It's hard to tell what. I'll look into their relationship dynamic a bit more, but unfortunately there are only two people who know for sure how it played out, and one's dead and the other isn't saying a word."

"Um, actually... she did say a few words."

His brows shot up. "When was that?"

"At the end. When we were leaving. She asked me to figure out who did this to Delphelius, because..." I shivered remembering. "She said she wanted to thank whoever it was."

"No kidding?"

"I wish I were. It was creepy."

"Sounds like it. But is she being clever or is what she said a sign that she really didn't do it?"

I shrugged. "She didn't seem upset about it happening, that's for sure."

He let out a deep breath like he was deflating.

"Thankfully *wanting* someone to be murdered isn't a crime, or else I'd never get a moment's rest. You may not know it, Miss Wildes, but you've been incredibly helpful here."

"I don't see how."

"I don't see how yet, either. But if there's one thing I know about investigations, it's that every little bit of insight proves helpful eventually, even if you can't see how right away. The last thing I want to do here is narrow in on a suspect too soon, especially one like Naomi where things don't quite add up. For instance, no one Tanner talked to on the patio last night saw her hanging around leading up to the murder. Everyone said they saw an elf stomp out of the pub and head off into the night. Nobody recalls seeing her come back."

That was interesting. "Is there a magic that elves possess that could allow her to murder someone from afar?"

"The elves are tight-lipped about their powers, but from what I understand, they work with earth magic, and it tends to be gentler stuff. Using it for murder is strictly forbidden and could lead to being cast out. I don't even know if it's possible. I'll have to look into that. And if it is, it sounds like she might've just been angry enough to think it was worth it to kill him. Still," he added, "I don't feel like she's a strong enough suspect to focus in on her yet. I don't even feel good about detaining her past lunch. So that means we need to keep looking."

"We?"

Deputy Manchester nodded. "Yes. Me, Deputy Culpepper, Sheriff Bloom, if she has the time."

"Oh."

"And you, if you're up for it."

My cheeks grew warm. "Me? I don't know how—"

"Respectfully, Miss Wildes, you're selling yourself short and it's doing nobody any good. If you'll let that go for a bit, I could really use your keen powers to help us try to find some additional persons of interest in this. You're kind and unsuspecting. Perfect for the job. Ask around town, see what emotions you pick up from people when they talk about Delphelius. No matter how inconspicuous something may seem, if it tickles your intuition at all, I'd love to hear about it. Would you be interested in helping out that way?"

When Stu Manchester started off a sentence with "respectfully," he was the kind of person you believed. He *was* being incredibly respectful to me, even as he was sort of calling me out.

How could I say no, really? If I could help close this case, and if there was some part to play that only I could fill, I didn't see another option. Not a moral or responsible one, at least.

"Okay," I said, trying to sound confident. "I'll look into it."

Deputy Manchester nodded. "And be safe. Not to scare you, but you never know what might happen with a killer on the loose."

Chapter Five

I didn't sleep well that night. A dream of Naomi grabbing my wrist with that cruel look in her eyes had jolted me awake at just after three in the morning, and no matter how closely I snuggled up against Atlas, my heart continued to race. I may have snagged another hour of sleep after that before I had to get up to go to work.

Atlas picked up on my exhaustion immediately as I sat up in bed and stretched out my neck and shoulders.

"Couldn't sleep?" he asked.

"I had a bad dream."

"Was someone bopping you?"

I shook my head. "It was about Naomi."

He shook out his bed-flattened fur. *"I didn't trust her one bit."*

"She was certainly unsettling. I can't imagine staying married to someone who I disliked so much. They have divorce in Eastwind, right?"

"You're asking the wrong person. I've been here as long as you have. They don't have divorce in the Dead-woods. As far as I know, they hardly have marriage there, and if it doesn't work out, it's usually because one of the spouses ate the other."

"Eek," I said, rolling out my stiff shoulders. "I'm pretty sure witches and elves don't eat their spouses."

"You never know."

I thought back over the previous day and my conversation with Deputy Manchester. "Do you think I might be able to help solve this case?"

"Probably, but I don't like us getting involved in other people's messes. Seems like it's asking for trouble. Very unsafe."

"If I can help, I think I should, don't you?"

"No."

"Oh. Well, I do. My main question is whether I actually *can* help. I've never been anyone special for even a day in my life, and now the senior deputy in town is telling me I'm the only one who might be able to sort this out? It's a strange feeling."

Atlas jumped off the bed and did a big stretch. *"You should listen to that strange feeling. It usually means something bad's about to happen. Maybe we should take the day off work and spend it at Medium Rare instead."*

A bacon addiction really had my familiar by the scruff of his neck if he was asking to spend the day so close to the Deadwoods.

As I got dressed, I thought more about the case.

Mostly, I thought about the confrontation between Naomi and Delphelius in the pub. My mind kept going back to that moment of glee. Who had that come from? It still felt so sharp in my memory, so... significant. Had it come from Naomi? One might assume so, but it didn't feel quite right. She had been shooting off waves of emotion, certainly, but I was starting to understand something about emotions that I never had before. They were like stews. The base broth of any stew was crucial to the overall flavor, but the other ingredients—carrots, onions, herbs, and meats—were what determined what kind of stew it turned out to be. Each emotion was made up of a different combination of ingredients, but there was a broth beneath it all that seemed specific to the individual.

That didn't mean I knew what each person's broth was, but it did tell me one important thing about the altercation at the pub: I was pretty sure that the emotion of glee wasn't layered over the same baseline as the emotions of rage and fury that had so clearly come from Naomi. That indicated to me that it belonged to someone else. But who?

Dang, Deputy Manchester might be right. I might have an advantage with my powers when it came to piecing together this case.

When I stepped into the kitchen to prepare some breakfast, Nora was already there. One of her eyes drooped slightly as she stared out the kitchen window into the backyard, gnawing on a raw carrot.

"Good morning," I said gently, realizing that she was in the same clothes that she'd put on the day before.

"Huh?" She turned toward me, and it seemed to take a second before her brain registered what she was seeing. She paused with the carrot halfway in her mouth. "Oh right. It's morning. Good morning."

"Long night?"

She shook her head with a sigh. "Long day followed by a long night. Blasted Flufferbum listed Medium Rare as the best place for late-night eats in town. We had a crowd all night. *All night!* That's never happened in the history of Medium Rare. It's usually just Hendrix Hardy battling his insomnia in a booth and maybe one or two other weres who come in from the Deadwoods after a late romp. Honestly, we shouldn't even stay open all night normally, but it's more of a tradition and a public service that we do. But last night?" She stared back out the window. "Last night was a mess. We ran out of queso at eleven thirty *in the morning* yesterday. I had to make some excruciating deals with the cheesemaker to get more cheese on such short notice. He price-gouged me, too, the jerk." She chomped the carrot aggressively. "I can't wait until these tourists leave."

"Maybe the murder will scare them away," I said.

She turned back toward me. "Delphelius Twench, right?" When I nodded, she said, "I heard Stu called you into the sheriff's. You helping them with the investigation?"

"As much as I can. I think you'd be better suited to the job. Your Insight is way more honed than mine."

"Nuh-uh," said Nora, waving the stub of her carrot at me. "You're not dragging me into an investigation right now. I think I have enough of a mess on my hands without solving the murder of some barfly nobody liked anyway. If Stu needs a Fifth Wind, you're on your own. Leave me out of it." She finished her carrot and, while she was still chewing, said, "Now if you'll excuse me, I'm going to slip into a coma for a few hours and hope Bryant can keep the diner from burning down until I make it back."

With the way she wobbled as she left the kitchen, I wondered briefly if she'd even make it to her bed before falling asleep.

One thing was clear now, though. I was the only Fifth Wind available for this job. Would my powers be enough? Or would I be the reason a killer slipped through the cracks?

Chapter Six

As it turned out, I would be up to my neck in tourists that day, too, and thoughts of the homicide would be knocked clean out of my mind by the chaos of the shop being under siege.

In the time since I'd left Time to Kiln the day before and when I'd opened it earlier that morning, word had apparently gotten around that it was one of the better shops to visit. Hardly any of the tourists were actually buying anything, but they were crowding into the space and making me exceptionally nervous about so many elbows near the pottery.

Atlas wouldn't even stay behind the desk with me and had opted instead to head into the studio and share Givens's big, fluffy cat bed. (I use the word "share" loosely, because Atlas took up all of it and then some, and Givens eventually gave up trying to claim a small corner and instead opted to curl up on one of the chairs in the break room.)

My anxiety about the elbows proved to be well-founded just after one in the afternoon, when the post-lunch crowd, no doubt foggy-headed from overeating and possibly having a pint with the meal, packed into the shop and I heard a large crash take place by the front window. I was explaining to a posh witch about the glazing process at the studio and why the particular mug she was examining cost as much as it did when the sound of shattering ceramics caused me to jump. By the time I made it to the mess, nobody was taking responsibility for it. We didn't have a you-break-it-you-buy-it policy in place, but that was mostly because we never needed it. Occasionally a child would break something, but Raven and Jude liked children too much to care about that, and the parents were always relieved when they learned that they wouldn't be emptying their pockets to cover their child's typical behavior.

But today, I didn't see a single child in sight. Only a bunch of adults looking in every direction by the shattered scrying bowl on the floor, distancing themselves from taking any responsibility whatsoever. It was one of those times when I wished I had it in my blood to be more confrontational, to say, "Okay, who did this? Fess up like the adults you supposedly are!" But I wasn't there yet. Maybe one day.

The accident did lead to many of the tourists slipping out of the shop, perhaps realizing for the first time that they were in danger of knocking something off the shelves themselves with this many people packed in. It gave me some space to retrieve the broom and dustpan and return to pick up the pieces.

As I was bending over the mess, Raven spoke up from behind me. "Let me get that." She waved her wand, and the pieces showed themselves into the dustpan. "I'll see if I can repair it, but honestly, that thing's been sitting on display for almost two years and no one's bought it. I'm not too worried about fixing it."

She was able to clean up all the bits with her magic at least twice as quickly as I would've the non-magical way, so I thanked her for the help.

"Don't mention it," she said, staring vaguely out the front window at the bunches of tourist groups.

"You okay?" I asked, picking up on her distraction.

She shook her head and looked at me, pushing a strand of her purple hair away from her face. "Yes, yes. I just... I keep thinking I recognize some of these tourists. Have you ever had a day like that? Where you keep thinking you recognize people who you couldn't possibly know?"

"Yes," I said, "I actually have. It was before I came here, though. Back home, there were so many people in my city that I mostly didn't know the people I passed on the street. But some days it was like that, my brain would tell me, *Oh, I know that person!* and then I would realize that I didn't. Just a split second of recognition. Is that what you're talking about?"

"Maybe." She appeared to slip back into her reverie, though. "No, it must be that. There's one person in particular who I swear I know from somewhere."

"Out there?" I pointed to the tourist group.

"No, not one of them. I saw him around town a couple of times yesterday."

"And you're sure he's not an Eastwinder?"

She shrugged. "I'm not sure. I don't think he lives here, but I've never been to Avalon, and most of these tourists are from there, so I don't know."

"Maybe he's visited Eastwind before," I suggested.

"Possibly." She shook her head and smiled. "It's probably nothing. Oh! You went and spoke with Deputy Manchester yesterday. Anything interesting come up?"

"Not particularly," I lied. "He asked me to keep my eyes and ears open for anything I may hear around town."

"You won't hear much about Delphelius," she said. "He was one of the most uninteresting people around."

"You knew him? I mean, more than you might know anyone in Eastwind?"

She nodded. "We were in the same class at Mancer Academy. When I tell you he peaked in school, I mean it. He thought he was such a hotshot witch. And he was fairly talented at magic, but it all went to his head. I don't think he could handle life after graduation, when nobody was around to stroke his ego about how great he was. I think it got to him. It happens from time to time around here. People get stuck in a time of their lives when everything was easy, and then they never bother learning how to live when things aren't handed to them. Delphelius was one of those people if I ever met one. Stalled out completely as an adult."

"And when did he and Naomi get married?"

"Right out of the academy," said Raven. "Before it was clear he was going nowhere. He was one of the most talked about witches at the time, which is likely the only reason an elf would consider him. I have nothing against elves, but they tend not to marry outside of their own kind."

"Did you know Naomi back then, too?"

"No, elves don't attend Mancer. I never heard of her until she and Delphelius began dating. She seemed obsessed with him. Big, doting eyes that she kept locked on him. He wasted no time proposing, and I think they made it about a year before the cracks really began to show in the relationship."

"And what did that look like?" I asked.

"He started spending more time at Sheehan's Pub without her, and she was rarely seen out and about. Spent most of her time at their home in Erin Park, tending to the garden. It's quite a nice garden. But I'm sure she missed living in Tearnanock Estates with her family. I've obviously never been allowed to visit that place—they're not particularly witch-friendly—but I hear the gardens are exceptional. Greener than anything one could cultivate in Erin Park."

"They must've been married for a long time, then," I

said, then, quickly realizing what was implied by that, I added, "Not to say you're old, but—"

Raven grinned. "No offense taken. My age comes as no surprise to me, so there's no harm in pointing it out. Yes, they were together about twenty-five years, if my math is correct."

"Why do you think they stayed together that long if their marriage started falling apart so early on?" I asked. "People can get divorced here, right?"

Raven chuckled. "Oh, absolutely. And they do all the time. Usually one of the partners moves to Avalon or some other realm so they don't have to run into their ex all the time but separating and divorce are certainly options. As to why Naomi and Delphelius decided to stay together, I couldn't tell you. If I had to guess about him, I'd say he married an elf specifically because he knew she wouldn't age like a witch would. She looks significantly younger than her age, if you haven't noticed. I suspect it helped him maintain the illusion that he was still at his peak, that he hadn't become a grown-up witch with a sad life and a drinking problem."

It was a more straightforward description of Delphelius than I would've gone with, but I couldn't say it was incorrect from what little I knew of him. "Why did Naomi stay with him so long?"

Raven let out a puff of air. "No idea, frankly. You'd have to ask her."

"I doubt she'd answer. She wasn't saying much of anything yesterday."

Raven's eyes shot open. "You spoke with her?"

Oops. "Um, not really. I mean, I was there when Deputy Manchester was asking her some questions, but she didn't say anything."

"But she's a suspect?"

Oh boy. I remembered Deputy Manchester's request to keep things quiet, and I'd already slipped up. Time to downplay. "I think they call it a 'person of interest,' but the spouse always is, right? And besides, I think they have a few things that point to it not being her."

"Then who could it be? Who else would've wanted to kill Delphelius?"

I shrugged. "No idea. I think that's why there hasn't been an arrest yet. The deputies are still looking into it."

She gave me a sideways glance. "Fair enough."

"If you think of anyone who might have a reason to kill Delphelius, I bet Deputy Manchester would like to know," I added.

"I'll think about it. I can imagine why someone wouldn't be particularly fond of a drunk like Delphelius, because he didn't give you much to like, but it still baffles me that anyone would hate him enough to kill him. He didn't do enough of anything to earn that sort of ire. Action outside of lifting a tankard to his lips wasn't quite his style."

Raven had a point, and I let it simmer in my mind as she went to work on some projects in the studio.

I tended to start from a place of liking someone until they gave me a strong enough reason not to like them, but

I understood that not everyone worked that way. Some people started from a place of not liking someone until they were provided a reason to the contrary. Not necessarily disliking the person, but simply feeling neutral. Most people stayed in that range of liking someone a bit, feeling neutral about them, or only slightly disliking them. Most people never got to the point of rage with others, let alone murderous rage.

But Delphelius had driven someone to that point, and despite the witnesses claiming they saw Naomi leave the pub and not return, she was the only person I knew of who had displayed the rage needed to want to take a life. And yet... that wave of glee I'd felt.

She was the top suspect, but deep down I felt certain for reasons I couldn't explain that it wasn't her. Who else could it be?

Chapter Seven

I was more than happy to finish my shift and hand the reins of the shop over to Sasha Cosmo for her shift. I had plans with Grace and Dante that afternoon about ten yards away from the shop at the pottery wheels in the studio.

The three of us set up in the center of the rows facing each other, with Dante on my left and Grace across from me. She had taken a break from her dinner plates and was working on a bird feeder, since Monty had taken an interest in birds after his visit to the Dead-woods, where he met Ted's flock of phoenixes. She had plans to set the bird feeder up in a tree in their backyard for Monty to enjoy—out of his five-year-old reach, since young werewolves did have a tendency to want to take an exploratory bite out of whatever small animals they could catch.

Dante was creating a series of eight dinner plates,

appetizer plates, and bowls for Ansel and Jane's wedding anniversary, which coincided with the Lunasa Festival. It was big project made more difficult by trying to match the sizes of each, and it was taking all his focus. Meanwhile, I was working on... another mug. I struggled to manage a lump of clay more than a pound and a half, and so I was mostly confined to smaller pieces like mugs. It was fun playing around with the body shape, giving it some flat edges or nice curves like a fertility goddess statue. I wasn't sure I was getting any better lately, but perhaps that wasn't the end goal.

Dante grunted and smashed a flat palm down onto the bowl on his wheel. The force sent a splash of slip onto my leg. "Sorry," he said.

I smiled at him. "Yes, I would hate to leave the wheel dirty." As always, I was absolutely covered in wet clay already.

The sarcasm seemed to cheer him, and he cleared the failed bowl from the wheel, grabbed another wedged lump of clay, and smacked it down in the center to start over.

Givens, the gray tabby who was the resident cat in charge of keeping small critters away, seemed to have developed a sense for when emotions were running high at the wheels. While he spent most of his days sleeping in sunbeams or on his overstuffed bed, moments like this would draw him in, and he'd rub up against the legs of the upset individual, offering a bit of support.

Dante leaned over and patted Givens on the head

with a clean elbow, and the cat purred appreciatively. Givens also muttered, *"Never thought I'd want to get this close to a werebear,"* but only I could hear him say that.

Grace paused her wheel, leaned to the side to check the shape of the center of her bird feeder, then dove right into the topic that I knew she'd been wanting to broach since we first met up in the studio a half-hour earlier. "It was someone at the pub, most likely."

I didn't have to ask her *what* was someone at the pub. There was no point playing coy here. Grace loved hearing gossip, but she wasn't one to spread it.

As for trusting someone with confidences, everyone deserves to have one person they tell everything to, no filter. And that one person doesn't tell anyone else, but knows that you're their one person, too. Dante was my one person. Now that Dante and I had made our relationship official, we didn't keep anything from each other. He told me all the gossip he heard around Franco's Pizza each day—which was a lot, as with any restaurant —and I told him whatever I'd learned from overheard conversations.

I'd never considered myself a gossip before coming to Eastwind, but that might've been because I had no one to gossip to nor anything to gossip about. Eastwind showed me a new side of myself.

However, I'd learned a few things about gossip. For one, it was useful when it came to keeping people safe. For instance, everybody knew that if the hobgoblin on Fluke Mountain invited you to his hut for an afternoon tea, you ought to say no if you didn't want to end up in a cauldron. Without gossip, how would people learn that if not the hard way?

But I also learned that I was fascinated by gossip in a way I hadn't appreciated before. To learn the strangeness of people I liked didn't make me like and respect them any less. If anything, it made me respect them more, as I was able to view them as unique, complex people who were so much more than the image they presented in public.

On top of that, I discovered that I didn't enjoy gossiping as much as I enjoyed being gossiped to. It was like having someone read you a book of vignettes, a peek into the lives of others that allowed me to recognize my own foibles. I didn't mind telling Grace things, because she usually had such a clear perspective to offer, and I loved telling Dante about things, because it tended to be the most animated I saw him, on those evenings we spent by the fire, rehashing our day. Outside of these two, though, I learned that I didn't much appreciate gossip outside of an investigation.

Or maybe I was just flattering myself. What was a murder investigation if not an opportunity to indulge in the most distillated, high-octane form of gossip?

I confirmed Grace's statement. "I do think it was someone at the pub."

"And not Naomi?" she said.

"Right. She left and no one saw her return prior to Delphelius stumbling into the side alleyway."

Dante removed his hands from the clay and looked up. "Are we sure it was a murder? Not some sort of freak accident where Delphelius tripped and hit his head?"

"I don't think it was that specifically," I replied. "I didn't get a look at the body, but Deputy Manchester did, and he didn't mention any possibility of a head injury. But I guess we won't know for sure until the medical examiner and magical examiner conclude their tests."

"I don't think it was an accident," Grace replied. "The timing doesn't make sense. He gets publicly humiliated by his wife and then simply dies without foul play?"

"Maybe he was embarrassed to death," Dante suggested.

"Doubt it," said Grace. "If you'd seen him, you'd know he appeared shameless about the whole thing."

"I have to agree with Grace on that," I said. "He didn't seem particularly affected by Naomi's yelling. I have a feeling there was a lot of yelling taking place in that marriage. But also... when it happened, I sensed this strange emotion..." I filled them in on the glee and how I was pretty sure it wasn't Naomi's.

"That only confirms it for me," said Grace. "It was someone in the pub who did it. They saw Delphelius get chewed out, and they were excited about it. If I saw someone I hated get publicly chewed out, I'd probably feel that way, too. It's not flattering to admit it, but it's true."

"Same," said Dante.

"Just because someone was glad to see it happen doesn't mean that the *murderer* was the one who was glad to see it happen," I said. "Maybe a lot of people had reason to hate Delphelius. Raven says she went to school with him and he was pretty insufferable. It doesn't seem like he's done a one-eighty with his personality since then, does it?"

"You're right," Grace offered. "There might've been multiple people who were glad to watch his wife hand it to him, but I still think that the best approach to narrowing down the pool of people to a few suspects is to think about who was at the pub. Or who was there around the time he left for the alley..." She chewed her bottom lip, and I could tell she was forming a theory.

"Who are you thinking of?" I asked.

"Well," she said, "Jaymes Hardy came inside not long after Delphelius disappeared from his place at the bar, right? It wouldn't take that long to kill a drunk man who presumably had his breeches down to urinate, right?"

I was rarely skeptical of Grace's theories, but this one struck me as somewhat out of nowhere. "Jaymes? Why on earth would he want to kill Delphelius? Or anyone? He seems like a good kid."

"Oh, I know Jaymes," said Dante. "He's a weird guy. I don't know about committing a murder or why he would hate Delphelius, but he's definitely strange."

"What do you mean?" I asked, surprised to find that I felt somewhat protective of the kid.

Dante shrugged. "Something's just a little off about him."

"He's obsessed with death," Grace said.

"What does that mean?" I asked.

"He talks about it all the time, and I've seen him in the necromancy section of the Pixie Mixie multiple times while I was in there gathering my own supplies."

"Oh come on, that doesn't mean anything. I've had to shop in the necromancy section of the Pixie Mixie, too, for my lessons with Nora."

Grace and Dante shared a quick look like two parents trying to maintain patience with a slow child. "Of course you're in the necromancy section," Grace said slowly. "You're a necromancer."

"Jaymes isn't even a witch," Dante explained. "The only things a werewolf would need would be basic medicinal herbs, and even then, I'm pretty sure they grow all of that out at the Scandrick compound."

"Is that what this is about?" I asked. "Not to accuse either of you of prejudice, but could some of your mistrust be about the fact that he's from the Scandrick compound?"

Grace shook her head, but Dante said, "Could be. Have you ever been out there? Of course not everyone who comes out of there is a little strange, but it's a rough place, and rough places can make strange people."

"I still don't know about him as a possible suspect," I said. "There's no motive. As far as we know, he has no more motive to kill Delphelius than anyone else in town. Or even one of the tourists!"

"Not everyone's as death obsessed as Jaymes," Grace said.

I felt myself getting prickly. "I wish you wouldn't call it death obsessed. Maybe he's just a little death... interested. Even in my own realm, that was something people his age got into."

"I suppose that's true," Grace said. "He is around the developmental stage where the prefrontal cortex begins to reach maturity, causing us to decentralize our experience as the center of the universe and realize that the world existed before us and will continue once we're dead. Perhaps he's just dealing with his own mortality in a somewhat morbid way."

"Exactly," I replied, not quite understanding what she'd said.

"But that still doesn't explain," she went on, "why he looks at you and Nora like you're goddesses."

Dante perked up. "What?"

"I don't know what you mean," I said. Although I did know what she meant. I saw the way he looked at Nora, though I hadn't realized that he looked at me the same way.

"I think he even came to Sheehan's specifically to find you," she added matter-of-factly.

"Grace!" I said, feeling myself blush. Dante was watching me closely, but I didn't dare look to my left at him.

Grace laughed. "What? It's true. I think he has a crush on you."

I waved her off. "No, no, no. Maybe he's fascinated with necromancy, like you said with the brain thing, but to be fair, it's not an uncommon obsession. For instance, when I was following Delphelius's ghost out of the pub, I ran into one of the tour guides, and he looked me up and down like he wanted to make me his lunch. All he said was that I was one of the Fifth Winds." A shiver ran down my spine at the memory. "It's not my favorite, but it does happen from time to time. People are fascinated by death. That doesn't mean they want to be the driving force behind someone dying."

I'd stopped listening to my own protestation, though, as it fell flat toward the end. There was no oomph behind it at all.

Because now that I thought about it, yes, the tour guide with the gaudy cerulean hat was walking *inside* just as I was walking *outside* to find Delphelius's body. And what had Raven said? She thought she recognized people from the tour group?

My mind sifted through the possibilities. There was far more to investigate with this. I might even have landed on a new possible suspect. But if so, maybe Deputy Manchester was right. Maybe it was time to shut the portal so the one responsible couldn't escape into Avalon.

Maybe it was time to lock ourselves in with a killer.

Chapter Eight

Deputy Manchester slipped into the seat I'd saved for him at the counter of Medium Rare. He was still in his uniform, since technically his shift had a few more hours to it, and he looked tired. "Miss Wildes," he said, nodding.

"Thanks for meeting me here, Deputy Manchester."

"Please, call me Stu."

"Um, okay. And you can call me Dahlia."

"No," he said, "I won't be doing that, Miss Wildes."

Jaymes hurried over on the other side of the counter to greet us. "Hi there, Dahlia! Can I start you off with some coffee? Chips and queso?"

It was dinnertime, so the coffee was out for me, but I smiled at him and said, "Water and some queso would be great." I made a show of turning to Stu, because Jaymes seemed like he might completely overlook the deputy.

"I'll take a coffee to start," said Stu.

Jaymes nodded and bolted off to get the order started.

"I'll be honest with you, Miss Wildes. We don't have much to go on in the investigation right now. Deputy Culpepper spoke with everyone at Sheehan's that night and was only able to rule out a few of the folks, like Ted."

"Ted would never kill someone," I said.

"Exactly. I don't know that he can, magically speaking. Hence ruling him out. As much as I'd like to rule out those who were accounted for in the bar from the time Delphelius left to the time he was found dead, I can't. Maybe someone slipped something in his drink that took a few minutes to set in. Maybe someone put a curse on him. We just don't know. Everyone who was seen there could be a person of interest, along with all kinds of folks who *weren't* seen there. Someone might've been waiting in the alley, say. One of the many joys of investigating murders in Eastwind is struggling to narrow down suspects."

I chewed on my lip, considering it. "I can see that."

"Maybe the MEs will come back with something soon. Cause of death or traces of magic. That would be a good start. But in the meantime, there might be some evidence that only you can gather for us."

"I know what you're talking about, but again, emotions can only get us so far. Just because someone's feeling guilt or rage doesn't mean we can attribute it to any one thing."

Stu nodded. "I understand that. But if we could rule out even just a few more people, I'd be much obliged for your help, Miss Wildes. Sheriff Bloom isn't big on the idea of shutting down the portal. I'm sure she understands it's the smart thing to do, but the High Council will make a headache of themselves about it, what with its possible impact on the tourism that's currently padding the town's pockets."

Jaymes plopped a cup of water and Stu's coffee down in front of us. "You ready to order?"

It was clear he didn't intend the plural "you" because he was only looking directly at me. Sheesh, had Grace been onto something? He certainly did have a penetrating stare with those dark brown eyes of his.

I looked at Stu, who nodded. Of course he was ready to order. He probably knew the menu better than Jaymes did.

Once we finished that business, and Jaymes assured me the chips and queso would be out soon, we were able to get back to our conversation. I was glad about that. As much as I hated to admit it, I was uncomfortable under those intense eyes of the young werewolf. It didn't mean he was a murderer, of course, or that he even made sense as a suspect, but I certainly made a note of it all the same.

"Where were we?" said Stu. "Ah yes, you were talking about the tourism. You have any reason to believe it might be a tourist who killed Delphelius? Or are you leaning more toward a local?"

It was so strange having a deputy ask *me* for my

opinion on the matter that I was tempted to say nothing. But perhaps anything, however logically unfounded it was, would be more helpful than nothing.

"I can't say exactly, but it's possible it was a tourist. They're not exactly the most ruly bunch, are they? I saw one puking his guts out at Sheehan's the other night. Couldn't handle a single night out at a pub. Seems like they could all use better chaperones."

"I'm inclined to agree with you there," said Stu. "But with regards to murder?"

"With regards to murder, I do have this strange tickle in the back of my mind..."

"I always appreciate a Fifth Wind's intuition, you know that, right? No matter how strange it sounds, I'd like to hear it. It usually turns out to be not so strange at all."

I felt the sincerity of his words, so I risked it. "Raven Goode said she was having this odd feeling where she kept thinking she recognized some of the tourists. A moment of recognition, almost like a twitch. But then she couldn't place it and wrote it off. I've had that before myself."

Stu's brows pinched together. "I have too, actually. When I was younger, I took a trip to Wisconsin. Felt it there."

"Then let me ask you this: during the time you were feeling that, did you *actually* recognize someone who you hadn't expected to see?"

After a silent pause, his eyes went wide. "Yes, actually. I kept thinking I recognized people—there was that glimmer of familiarity, but it never panned out. Until that evening, when I ran right into Zax Banderfield, of all people, in a glade. He used to be the leader of the werebears, back before your time. Good man. I had no idea he was on vacation there too. Yet somehow a bear and an elk met in the middle of a glade within a thick and vast forest in a realm that wasn't their own, and they knew each other."

"Exactly," I said. "I've had the same experience a handful of times, even before coming to Eastwind. On those days when I kept thinking I recognized strangers, almost inevitably I'd end up running into someone familiar in a place I didn't expect to see them. It's like a part of me knew that would happen and was keeping me alert for it all day."

Stu nodded adamantly. "You believe Raven might truly recognize one of the tourists."

"I think it's possible."

"And what would that mean?" he asked.

It was the question I'd been knocking around in my mind since I'd spoken to her. "I don't know," I said. "But it strikes me as something to think about."

"Might as well," he concluded, as Nora carried over a large bowl of tortilla chips and the accompanying smaller bowl of queso and set them down in front of us.

"Siren's song, am I glad I don't have to be part of *this* conversation," she said. Then she added, "By the way, Atlas is in the kitchen, learning the hard way that anything Anton drops on the floor is going to be painfully hot to eat. Dunno if you were wondering where he'd disappeared to."

"I figured he was around here somewhere," I said. "I'll make sure he has cold water to drink tonight for his scalded tongue."

"Good call, because he doesn't seem to be learning the lesson. I just saw him swallow a strip of bacon whole while the grease was still popping and sizzling."

I cringed. "Should I go get him? Is he in the way?"

She waved me off. "Anton will give him firm nudge with his boot if he becomes a problem. Ogres don't tend to be intimidated by hellhounds, as Grim could tell you. He once tried to jump up and grab a burger patty right off the griddle when Anton had his back turned. He regretted that. Anton decked him right in the face." She laughed. "I just saw him sprinting out of the kitchen with his tail tucked between his legs. He didn't try that again."

I didn't like the thought of Atlas taking a hit from an ogre, especially if it set him back a few months in his fear of being bopped, so as loudly as I could through our mental connection, I said, *"Anton will kick you if you get in the way."*

A moment later, Atlas scooted out of the kitchen and went to hide behind the counter.

Nora arched a brow at me. "Must be nice to have a familiar who doesn't insist on learning every lesson the hard way." She grabbed one of the chips off the plate, dipped it, and crammed it in her mouth. "You two make any progress with the investigation?"

"I thought you didn't want to be part of the conversation," said Stu.

Nora shrugged. "I don't. But with each year I spend in this town, I become more and more of a busybody. Can't a gal just want the gossip without becoming part of every investigation?"

"A gal could," said Stu. "But I don't know that *you* can."

Nora glared at him. "For that, I'm *definitely* staying out of this one, just to prove you wrong. Well"—she turned to me— "good luck, and since the two of you are clearly at an impasse, or else you wouldn't be killing time together at a diner, let me offer you this one bit of wisdom, Dahl: be nosier." She stole one more chip and shoved it in her mouth as she walked away.

"She's not wrong," said Stu. "I have certain rules I have to play by as a deputy that a private citizen like you can skirt. Not to mention, everyone knows what I do for a living, so I can't exactly be discreet. You, on the other hand..."

I understood. Nora had explained as much about her role in investigations. Law enforcement had to answer to the High Council. But if a case was solved and the sheriff's department didn't break any rules itself, the High Council was unlikely to ask too many questions about how it went down.

"There are some things only a Fifth Wind can find,

too," Stu added. "Certain interviews that I can't conduct, for instance."

He didn't have to say more. I knew what he meant and what he needed from me. I wasn't sure if I could pull it off, but it was still up to me to try. I'd just have to be nosier.

Chapter Nine

Atlas loped by my side as I entered Sheehan's Pub later that evening. It was a completely different scene from the last time I'd entered. Almost no one was inside, and I spotted Fiona throwing scufflepuck with Oliver Bridge-water rather than engaged in the many tasks that usually preoccupied her at work.

When she spotted me entering, she started to make for the bar, but I waved her off. "I'm good for now," I said.

I wasn't here for a drink. I was here on a hunch. A hunch that, as it turned out, was right on.

There seemed to be a few small threads I could pull at insofar as suspects, although none of them felt substantive. But there was one source of information that was left to tap if I could tap it, and that was Delphelius himself.

His spirit was hunched over the bar on the same stool

where he'd wasted away most of his final years of life. I'd thought I'd find him there.

Atlas stayed close to my side as I slid onto the stool beside the ghost. I opened my mouth to start up a conversation, but when I realized I was about to ask, "How are you?" I decided it might be best to build rapport some other way with a murder victim.

"Remember anything new about who might've killed you?" I asked, which felt hardly less insensitive.

"Nope." A tankard sat on the counter in front of him, sweating down the sides. Did Fiona know he was there somehow, or had she merely left his usual drink in tribute? Either way, he reached for the tankard, wrapped his ghostly fingers around it, and raised his arm like he was bringing the drink to his lips. Obviously, the tankard stayed right where it was.

"Is he there?" Fiona called to me over her shoulder.

"Do you mind if I tell her?" I asked Delphelius.

He shrugged like he couldn't care less.

"Yes, he is."

"Is he saying anything?" Fiona replied.

"Not really."

She slid one last puck across the table and pumped her fist as it bashed into another puck, causing them both to explode in a puff of colorful smoke. I had no idea what the rules of scufflepuck were, but it seemed from Oliver's disappointed reaction that she'd pulled off quite a move.

She dusted her hands off and walked over. "I could never get him into a conversation, either. First time he came in, I couldn't even get him to tell me what he wanted to drink. He just pointed at the taps, and I poured him one. Been serving him the same kind of ale ever since. I would've switched it up if he ever asked me to, but he never did."

"He knows how to have a conversation, though, right?" I asked.

"Sure. But you have to know the right topic to get him started on."

I was stumped there. "Like what?"

Fiona winked at me. "Ask him about his time at Mancer Academy."

Ah, of course. I should've known from Raven's description of him. I turned to the ghost. "You went to Mancer Academy?"

The spirit blinked and finally lifted his drooping head, turning to look at me. "Of course I did. Surprised you would even have to ask. I ran that place back in my day."

This wasn't my first choice of topic—after all, it was years before he was murdered, and I wasn't exactly trying to make friends with him. I just wanted to get to the bottom of the case. But still, I'd learned over my years as a house cleaner that even the most unrelated and mundane topic could reveal interesting truths about a person. So I said, "What do you mean by 'you ran it'? You were the principal?"

He laughed. "I had the principal doing my bidding, so essentially yes. They'd never seen such a talented East

Wind witch. I heard as much from all my teachers. I could make a single water droplet expand into vapors of any shape and size. I could tap into the spring itself."

"The spring?"

"The one that runs below the town. You really don't know anything, do you?"

I was taken aback by the unnecessary jab, but I managed to keep from saying anything, and he was happy to go on.

"Fulcrum Fountain is spring fed. I used to be able to shape it however I wanted. I once turned the water from a jet into a braided rope and used it to trip Count Malavic as he walked through the park. If he'd ever found out it was me, he would've killed me."

"You think so?"

"Oh, sure. Or maybe he would've turned me into another vampire like him. No clue. He fell flat on his face, and three children saw it and started laughing. Glad they did, because me and my buddy couldn't keep from laughing, too, and their laughter covered up ours."

"Your buddy? Do they have a name?"

Delphelius shrugged. "Couldn't tell you. Never kept up with him. He wasn't very talented anyway. Sort of a burnout as soon as we graduated. Never made anything of himself."

The lack of self-awareness was certainly notable.

"Did you do that sort of thing a lot?" I asked.

"Of course. What else is there to do in this boring town? Even as a teenager, I knew it was a dull place to live. Nobody was as talented as I was, either. I think some might've been, if they'd tried. But nobody did. And I was a natural talent. I could summon the spring water up through the pipes and make it shoot out of the academy toilets as soon as someone sat down. Could bring up so much pressure that it'd knock them off the seat with their pants down."

Thankfully, he was so lost in those fond memories that he didn't notice the horror on my face. "That's interesting."

"It was, but eventually it lost its shine. There was this one kid, though, and no matter how many times I did it, it always got to him. He challenged me to a duel eventually. A South Wind, though, and you know how those pyromancers are. Only one trick up their sleeve. Oh, you gonna shoot some flames at me? Please. So he wants to duel me down at the graveyard, and I agree. He shoots some flames my way, but I'm ready, because again, pyromancers are generally uncreative and predictable. I douse his flame with water that I condense from the air around me and neutralize his attack. Then I counter with a jet stream that shoots at him so fast it takes his ear right off. He's lucky I wasn't aiming for his face. I wasn't mean, though. Not like that. I did want people to know who was the best, though. It's important for people to understand that and let the natural order be. Some of them tried to top me, you know. There were always other students challenging me, thinking they were better than me. It was so easy for me, though. One girl, a mousy little

North Wind, tried to tell me off, like I would care what she thought. I conjured up a bucket of cold water in the air above her and dumped it on her head. She looked like a soaked rat. Ran off crying."

I glanced over at Fiona, who had a knowing smile on her face. "What'd I tell you? I can tell just by the look on your face that you're hearing some of the stories he's told me."

I didn't want to get on Delphelius's bad side, not only because he seemed to be a bully at heart, but because I might need to ask him some further questions later. But I also didn't know how much more of his self-centered boasting I could take. Did he think I would be impressed by how he'd wielded his hydromancy against his classmates?

My mind flashed back to the words Naomi had spoken to me: "I want to thank whoever killed him."

Perhaps I was finally getting a glimpse into what their marriage was like. And if Delphelius thought there was nothing wrong with this behavior, then it was likely his classmates weren't the only ones who'd been on the wrong end of his bullying.

I'd come to Sheehan's with the hope that I would learn more about Delphelius's life and be able to pick out a few suspects. Instead, all I'd learned was that Eastwind might be chock-full of people with a motive to kill him.

The more I learned about the victim, the more suspects seemed to pop up, faceless people from his past, nameless because he'd never bothered to learn their names, let alone remember them.

But I bet they remembered *his* name. Was it possible that someone had kept it fresh in their mind for days, weeks, or possibly years, until the opportunity to get even had arrived?

Chapter Ten

The Pixie Mixie was still open when I was finally able to politely extricate myself from Delphelius's harrowing tales of his school days. I didn't think he even noticed that I was leaving. He would've bragged about his exploits to a wall, and indeed, that was what he continued to do as Atlas and I left the pub and walked the short distance to the apothecary.

"Not the nicest of people," Atlas said.

"Certainly not the nicest. I'm sure if I poked around a little bit more, we'd find some reason for it, though. Maybe his father was mean to him when he was little."

"You think that would change the way the people he bullied felt about him?"

I sighed. "Probably not."

Since I'd enjoyed an early dinner with Stu, the sun had hardly set by the time Atlas and I reached the Pixie

Mixie and stepped inside to the delicate sound of a tiny bell over the door.

Kayleigh Lytefoot, a beautiful fairy with golden hair and a generous smile, fluttered her wings and welcomed us in. "Dahlia! So nice to see you. Let me know if I can help you find anything. Oh! We restocked the sun-dried wormwood, if you still need it for your training."

"Maybe soon. I'm actually here to, um, ask you about something."

She fluttered higher above the ground so that we were at eye level once I reached the checkout desk. "Of course. Is this"—she narrowed her eyes slyly—"something to do with an ongoing investigation? Has Nora already passed the torch to you? No, of course she hasn't. She's far too addicted to the thrill of a case."

I laughed. "I think you're right about that, but she's been swamped down at Medium Rare."

"So this *is* about a case. Delphelius Twench, maybe?"

I'd been hoping I didn't have to disclose that, because I didn't want the questions I needed to ask to paint anyone as a suspect when they were hardly even a person of interest. "I'd rather not say," I replied, and Kayleigh nodded knowingly. "What I'm wondering about is if Jaymes Hardy has been in here lately, and if so, what he was shopping for."

"Is he a sus—" She caught herself, remembered she was supposed to be pretending that this wasn't about the Twench case, and continued, "I've seen him in here lately, but I don't usually disclose purchases to people. I like my customers to know that what they buy here, and what potions those supplies imply they might be making, are completely private."

"Could you at least tell me if, in your opinion, the items Jaymes bought the last time he was in here are the kind that would be used for some sort of spell, or if they were more everyday essentials for medicinal uses?"

She chewed on her bottom lip for a moment, and I could tell she wanted to say something but wasn't sure how best to approach it. That was a good sign. At least she knew something helpful. I wasn't great at being pushy, but maybe I could try it on for size here if I thought it might get me closer to understanding more about Jaymes.

"I don't believe it was solely medicinal," she said. I waited for more, but that was all she was willing to give me. So far.

Nora was known for the information she could get out of people in an investigation, but there was someone who was even better at getting people to talk, and so I asked myself, "What would Grace do?" The witch asked questions with such objective curiosity that I always found myself answering, even if the answer I gave was unflattering or embarrassingly honest. And I was always glad I'd answered in the end.

"Did you see him shopping in the necromancy section at all?" I asked, keeping a poker face like Grace would.

Kayleigh didn't have to say a word for me to know that she had. Shades of surprise were some of the most difficult for me to detect on others, but she was startled enough by my directness, and likely the fact that I already had some information to begin with, that I was able to pick up on her emotion. "I did see him over there. But I can't confirm that he bought any necromantic supplies."

"Got it," I said. My heart was racing from continuing to push this conversation. It felt like at any moment I could go too far and cross some boundary that hurt my casual relationship with her (and the last thing anyone would want to do is make the person who owns the apothecary dislike you). I liked Kayleigh, and I wanted her to like me back, but I also really needed to know more about Jaymes. I took a different tack.

"Let's say, hypothetically, that a werewolf comes in here and purchases a bunch of ingredients from the necromancy section. Would that seem strange to you in general?"

The fluttering of her wings became more relaxed. "It certainly would. Werewolves don't have the kind of magic that witches do. They can perform some basic recipes, but not necessarily spellwork."

"Nothing strong enough to kill a witch at a distance?" I asked.

"None that I know of. There is one exception, though." She hesitated, and I held my breath, hoping she would continue on her own. She did. "If the werewolf has a parent who's a witch, then sometimes they can inherit a little bit of that magic."

"Like Monty," I said.

"Can he do magic?"

"None that I've heard of, but he's only five. He's still learning how to control his shifting."

Kayleigh nodded. "Then there's still time. I wouldn't expect him to ever have the powers that Grace does, but he might have a little bit come through here and there. A werewolf with a witch's magic isn't completely unheard of." She leaned forward conspiratorially. "If I were to see a werewolf shopping in the necromancy section, I would definitely wonder who that werewolf's parents were."

I took the hint. This was as much as she could tell me, but it was plenty. "That sounds smart," I replied. "Someone ought to look into that, were a werewolf ever to start shopping in the necromancy section."

She bit back a mischievous grin. "Indeed. Someone ought to. Especially if there's an unsolved murder."

"Are there necromantic spells that can kill someone?" I asked. "I thought it was more for bringing the dead back to life."

"Necromancy is simply magic of the soul, dead or alive. It can do all kinds of things. Very powerful, some of them, which is why it tends to be viewed with suspicion. But as I'm sure you know, it doesn't have to be malevolent."

"I'm learning more about that every day," I said. "Maybe one day soon I'll understand myself."

Kayleigh giggled. "That's the dream, right? For us to one day understand ourselves enough to learn our full capacity. I've had centuries to figure it out, and I'm still a mystery to myself in many ways. Perhaps not the most urgent mystery for the time being, though." She winked.

Too true. I certainly needed to learn more about my powers, but for now, the mystery begging to be solved involved a murder, one with an unknown killer who might strike again at any time...

Chapter Eleven

It was just after nine when I left the apothecary. If I hurried, I could make it over to Franco's Pizza before they locked the doors. Atlas was more than happy to speed up his trot for the promise of whatever meatballs might be left over at the end of the day.

The restaurant closed at nine on weeknights, but the tables were still full when I arrived at five after. I went to open the door, and it was locked. Drat. The loudest voice inside me said not to be a bother and simply to go by the next day once I got off my shift at Time to Kiln. I thought about listening to the voice. But then I spotted Dante through the window, and before I could stop myself, I waved him down. He grinned when he saw me and let me inside without a second thought.

"Sorry to bother you," I said. "I promise I'm not going to order something and upset the kitchen. Is Jane here?"

"All business, huh?" he said playfully.

"Oh, right." I offered him a quick peck on the cheek. "Sorry. It's been a long day."

"You're clearly on a mission, so I understand. Jane's counting the receipts in the back. I'll go get her for you."

"Only if it's not too big of a pain," I said. "It's still crazy in here."

"If this is about Delphelius, then you get to put people out, Dahlia. Sort of worth it, don't you think?" He ignored one of the tables trying to wave him down and led me over to the bar. "Stay here and I'll go get her."

I parked on one of the high stools and told Atlas to stay next to me. "This isn't Medium Rare," I reminded him. "You can't go around begging for scraps. This is a classy establishment, and I don't think Jane would appreciate it."

"I bet she would. It might run some of these tourists out of here."

He had a point, but I wouldn't concede that. I wanted him to stay with me for now.

Jane came out of the back carrying a plate of meatballs. "They're a little cold," she said, sliding them across the counter to me. "And one's been bitten into." She rolled her eyes. "One of these tourists was shocked and appalled to learn that our meatballs were seasoned. She said it was spicy. Spicy! Rosemary, oregano, garlic, salt, and a little crushed pepper flakes, and she can't handle it. I don't know what kind of bland food they're getting in Avalon, but we don't do that here."

I set it down for Atlas, who didn't seem to mind the

room-temperature meat at all. It certainly wasn't too spicy for him.

"Dante said you wanted to ask me a few questions. What can I help you with, Nora? Oh, I mean Dahlia." She winked at me.

I wasn't as slick about my intentions as I'd hoped, but fair enough. "Do you know much about Jaymes Hardy's parents?"

She didn't appear to have expected that question, and she pouted as she considered it. "His mother is Geena Hardy, Hendrix Hardy's little sister. Not sure who his father is. Anything's possible out in the Scandrick compound. That's why I left it as soon as I got the chance."

"Do you know Geena?"

Jane arched a brow at me. "You think every werewolf knows every other werewolf in this town?"

"Oh, sorry," I said quickly. "I don't mean—"

She held out a hand to stop me. "It's fine. We do. I grew up with Geena. She lived down the street from me. As far as Hardys went, she seemed fairly well adjusted. The whole family has sleep issues. Hendrix's insomnia is one of the more desirable conditions. Geena sleepwalked sometimes, but she usually ended up back at her house, no harm done. She had another brother, Felix, though, and he would scream so loud in his sleep that it woke up the whole block. He also sleepwalked a little bit, but when he did, something was usually set on fire." She shrugged. "Like I said. Geena seemed normal by association."

"And you don't know who Jaymes's father is?"

"Nope. Never heard anyone talk about it. Presumably Geena knew, but she took that to the grave."

"She's dead?"

"Yeah. About a year ago. Not sure what happened."

"Were she and Jaymes close?" I asked.

Jane shrugged. "No idea. Nora might know better. I don't talk to the kid. In fact, I suggested Nora reconsider hiring him, but she was desperate. I wouldn't hire him here. Strange one, Jaymes. Just something off about him. If you think he had something to do with Delphelius's murder, I wouldn't blame you."

"What? Oh. No, I'm not..."

"Okay, sure," said Jane incredulously. "Anything else you needed to ask me?"

"No. You've been helpful. Thanks."

"No, thank you for taking a burden off my best friend by doing this. I've been telling Nora for years that she needs to stop trying to juggle these sorts of cases with owning the diner, but she won't listen to me. I'm glad you're here. Dante?" Dante looked up from where he was mixing a drink farther down the bar. "Comp whatever she wants to drink."

"Was already planning on it," he said. "You think I'm gonna let my girlfriend pay for her own drinks?"

Jane laughed. "Ansel's the same way. I keep telling

him I make more money than he does, but werebear men won't hear it."

Dante brought me over a chilled glass of white wine a moment later and leaned his elbows on the counter. "I heard you asking her about Jaymes. You finally believe he makes a solid suspect?"

"I never said that. I'm just being open and curious." I paused. "Do you think Delphelius ever went down to the Scandrick compound? Maybe twenty-two years ago?"

He eyed me closely. "That's an interesting question."

"It certainly is. One I didn't think I would have to ask."

"Hey!" came a stern voice from behind me. "Can we get some service over here?"

I turned and was not surprised to see the increasingly familiar face of the tour guide glaring at Dante.

"I'm not even their server," he muttered to me, before pushing himself up off the counter and heading over to the table.

I watched him go, but mostly, I kept my eye on the tour guide. Today's hat was a feathery emerald-green monstrosity, like a tropical bird had fallen from the sky and splatted on the ground.

I tuned in and felt suppressed anger seeping from Dante. The tour guide was difficult to read, though. It was definitely a strong flavor of emotion he felt, but it was one I hadn't gotten around to practicing on. Entitlement? Superiority? Inferiority? I wasn't sure.

But I did get a prickle from what I suspected was my

newfound power of Insight, and it told me to finish my drink quickly enough that I could follow this group out. There was something about the tour guide and his dozen or so tourists that kept nudging at me every time I saw them. And it wasn't just his poor taste in hats. Something else was there. Of all the tour groups in Eastwind right now, I kept running into *them*. Coincidence, or something magical conspiring for it to happen?

Only one way to find out.

Chapter Twelve

I followed the tour guide and his group as they left Franco's. While I loved having Atlas with me as a deterrent against anyone trying anything, his presence also assured me that I couldn't be as incognito as I'd have liked. I'd have to make it work.

One of the group, a leprechaun dressed in a fancy frock that you'd never see any Eastwind leprechaun caught dead in, addressed the tour guide. "Lifton, you said yesterday that the Deadwoods had a fierce reputation and we wouldn't be venturing in during our time here. Is that true?"

The tour guide—Lifton, apparently—raised his chin and spoke with complete confidence. "It's true. No one who has entered the Deadwoods has ever returned."

I paused and shared a quick look with Atlas. The Deadwoods were certainly no playground for unsupervised young witchlings, but people made it out of there all the time. Grace and Landon had just brought Monty in there to visit Ted and made it out okay. Heck, even I had started my Eastwind residency there and wandered out unharmed.

The leprechaun nodded appreciatively, and didn't ask any further questions about the forest. The rest of the group happily accepted the response, too.

Lifton the tour guide was, apparently, full of unicorn swirls. Did he know that he was wrong about the Deadwoods? And if he did, did he care? It was certainly an interesting development.

I continued to follow at enough of a distance that I wouldn't draw attention to myself, but close enough that I could pick up on snippets of the conversation. Lifton was so surrounded by the interested hodgepodge of tourists, who seemed to hang on his every word, that I was unable to get a clear read on any emotions he might've been feeling.

I followed them as they made for the center of town. Before we emerged from the side street, Lifton pointed to one of the run-down buildings and said, "Remember when I told you about the Werewolf Rebellion? That's where the first slash of claws happened."

"And they turned it into a butcher shop?" one of the tourists asked, pointing toward the sign above the door.

"That's just a cover. You'd be shocked how many of these so-called local businesses are trafficking fronts."

I felt personally offended, hearing him throw around accusations like that without a single grain of truth behind them. Sure, I didn't know everything that happened around town, and maybe there were some illegal magical supplies being trafficked, but to assume the butcher shop was a part of it and to cast doubt on every other business...

It was rare that I took a strong dislike to someone, but I was certainly not a fan of Lifton and becoming less of one with each unfounded story he told.

"And see that window there?" He pointed vaguely toward one of the two-story brick buildings that housed many of the merchants, due to its proximity to the Eastwind Emporium. It was anyone's guess what window, specifically, he was pointing to, and he probably didn't know. "It was out of that window that a werewolf leapt upon an elf named Felinity Featherwhite and tore her to shreds. Law enforcement said that he had been stalking her for months, prowling behind her and following her trail. He murdered the inhabitant of that apartment so that he could gain access to the window, knowing that she frequently took this exact route from Medium Rare to her home in Erin Park."

"Why did he do it?" asked a plump older woman.

"Nobody knows," Lifton replied.

I had a feeling that nobody knew because it had never actually happened. It was simply a sensational story told to make Lifton seem like he knew the town well.

"And how long ago did this happen?" asked another tourist.

"Only five months ago."

The group ooh-ed and aww-ed at the freshness of the crime.

"For fang's sake," I muttered. I was already in Eastwind five months ago. I absolutely would've heard about that if it'd happened. Everyone would've.

Not only was Lifton a liar, but he was a risky one. If a single Eastwinder had overheard him telling that story, they would've called him out.

Then I realized that an Eastwinder *had* heard him tell that story. Me. Would I call him out? Unlikely. And maybe he knew that. Not specifically about me, but about people in general. Many would hear something like that, wrinkle their brow about it, then assume they misheard and continue on with their day. Someone like Dante or Grace might say something, but I wasn't like them. Besides, I didn't want to draw attention to myself. I needed to know more about this man. He was certainly into scandal and dark dealings, at least in the stories he told. It kept the attention of his group directly on him, too. Could he have gone farther than merely telling macabre stories about the town? Could he have created his very own by following Delphelius into that alley outside Sheehan's Pub?

As the group made its way into the Eastwind Emporium, which had shut down trade for the night so that the space was mostly open and silent, Lifton directed the group toward the clock tower.

"It looks so ominous," I heard one of the tourists mutter to another.

I couldn't have disagreed more. Seeing the face of the clock lit up at night always felt peaceful and calming to me. It reminded me of an ancient, kindhearted guardian that watched over the town day and night, never sleeping and always sharing its warm glow with whomever might need it.

But I could certainly see how someone who'd been listening to scary, made-up stories about the town all day —which seemed to be Lifton's specialty—might land on "ominous" as a descriptor.

A cluster of tourists were already gathered at the base of the clock tower, and I recognized the person standing in front of them, motioning upward. I didn't know Echo Chambers had gotten into the tourism game, though.

It wasn't too unpredictable, when I reflected on it, however. Echo was a businessman—how honest he was about it was sometimes up for debate—and always looking for a new way to cash in. The satyr owned a few establishments around town, mostly in the expensive shopping district. Echo's Salon was one of the places I dreamed of being able to afford. The satyr was one of the few people in Eastwind who had thick, curly hair like mine, and I held the belief that those working at the salon he owned might be able to give my curls a proper trim. But it was way outside of my price range.

Echo paused mid-sentence, his hands that had been gesturing falling to his side when he spotted the other group approaching. "Not you again," he spat at Lifton.

"Still boring these fine people out of their mind?" Lifton replied.

"They're not bored by the truth. Perhaps you'd find the same about your fine folks if you stopped making up tales for even five seconds."

Lifton rolled his eyes, and I noticed that both groups of tourists were looking progressively confused. I could feel a fog of unease spreading out around them. "Just because you don't have an inside line to the seedy under-belly of Eastwind doesn't mean that I'm not functioning completely on truth. Take this clock tower, for instance. Did you know that an elf jumped from it, plummeting to his death, nearly forty years ago?"

Echo blew a raspberry. "I think I would've heard about that. I am, after all, a local."

"Ah yes," said Lifton with a smirk. "How could I forget? I was just remembering the old days, back when both of us had some style and class. Some self-respect. Back before you started chasing clout rather than having any of it."

I'd never seen Echo look so furious in his life. His usual aloofness had evaporated completely, and suddenly I received a flash of an image from his point of view, as if seeing through his eyes as he charged Lifton and wrapped his hands around the man's throat.

I stumbled a half step back, steadying myself on Atlas. Oh wow, that was certainly new and interesting. In reality, Echo had done no such thing and was only staring furiously at the tour guide.

What was also interesting was that these two seemed to know each other. Maybe for a long time.

Lifton turned back to his group. "It's true, this clock tower is the site of a dangerous haunting that resulted from not one, but two elves jumping to their deaths."

"Did they know each other?" someone asked.

"They did. And it's said that they still haunt the clock tower to this day. If you gaze up there at midnight on a new moon, you can see them standing on the edge, preparing for their last moments. I've seen it myself."

"I've never heard such swirls in all my life," Echo spat. He clip-clopped angrily toward Lifton, getting in the man's face. "For one, there's no haunting in the clock tower. And for another, if there were, a mediocre witch like you would never be able to see it. That would take a Fifth Wind. Like her."

I shrank away as Echo pointed directly at where Atlas and I were hanging back in the shadows, doing our best but now failing to go unnoticed.

There was nowhere to hide, though, and Echo didn't let up. "Tell him, Daisy. There aren't any ghosts in the clock tower. Tell him he's so full of unicorn swirls that it's coming out of his ears."

I said nothing about him getting my name wrong. I could not possibly want to be involved in their beef any less. But all eyes were on me now, and I needed to say something. Anything. "I've never seen a ghost up there," I said. "But then again, I don't think I've ever been here at midnight on a new moon."

My diplomacy wasn't well met. Instead of avoiding getting involved, I'd only made Echo turn his anger my way. Yikes.

Lifton didn't seem bothered, though. Instead, he seemed pleased to notice that I was there with him. "You're the Fifth Wind I saw at Sheehan's Pub on the night of the murder, right?"

Oh boy. "I was there, yeah."

You would've thought winter solstice had come early with the way his eyes lit up. "And you saw the dead man's ghost."

I didn't like the greediness on his face. I was not a person to him, but a possible source to be tapped for his dark and twisted stories. Atlas's hackles rose and he pressed his ears back on his head.

"I didn't," I said quickly, the lie sounding unconvincing even to my own ears. "I didn't see any ghosts."

Lifton didn't let up. "Of course you did." He took a step closer to me. "You must've. You found the body, right? In the alley. Everyone was talking about it. You can't deny that you found it. And how else would you have known to look there if he hadn't told you?" His eyes were wide, and while I had a vague sense that everyone was listening to this interaction with bated breath, I couldn't tear my attention away from Lifton's greedy expression long enough to check. "What did he say to you? Anything useful?" He continued stalking closer to me, and the light from the clock tower cast long, dark shadows down his face. *"Did he tell you who killed him?"*

Atlas's fear response kicked in, and I was grateful that this time it was fight, not flight. The hellhound lowered his head and growled, showing Lifton sharp teeth.

The tour guide blinked and seemed to snap out of his locked-in state. "Spell's bells!" He covered his heart and took a step back. "Get your beast under control! This place really is full of bumpkins who resort most quickly to violence!" He retreated to the safety of his group, and I was so relieved to see it, I didn't take offense at his words.

"Good boy," I said silently to Atlas.

"I think I peed a little," he replied.

"I might've too. I don't like that man at all."

"I don't want to bite him. I bet he tastes sour."

I wove my fingers into the thick fur of his scruff. *"No biting tonight. I think you've made your position known."*

"The truth finally comes out!" declared Echo, turning everyone's attention away from me. "Your disdain for this town is finally clear. You're not a tour guide at all. Just a professional gawker. If I were your customer, I'd demand a refund."

I took the opportunity to move on, giving both tour groups a wide berth as the guides continued to bicker. Atlas stayed between me and the others, though I was pretty sure he'd sent a clear enough message that nobody would come close. I appreciated his extreme bravery all the same. No doubt he would crash as soon as we could make it home, which was the only destination I had in mind just then. We could curl up in bed, and I could hold him closely as his body shook from the stress of his courage. And I wouldn't mention that I noticed his shaking either.

I was glad to be back on a dark side street. Just the two of us. Nora and Tanner's house was a few blocks on, and I tried to slow my pace and take deep breaths to calm my beating heart. "Wow," I said finally, once I could return to myself. "I get a really bad feeling about Lifton. Like, really bad."

"We should tell someone. Let the deputies handle it. Maybe even Sheriff Bloom."

"That's smart. I don't think I want to be messing with him anymore. That look in his eyes when he asked me if Delphelius had told me who murdered him..." A shiver ran through my body. "I don't see how he would fit in with the case, but if you were to tell me that you found proof he was the one to kill Delphelius, I'd be inclined to believe you."

"If he didn't kill Delphelius, he might've killed someone else. Seems like the type."

"You're right," I said. "When he looks at me, it's like

he's not seeing *me*. He's seeing what I can do for him. I'm glad to be away from him."

"*You're feeling calmer now?*" he asked.

"Definitely."

"*Then I hate to be the bearer of bad news, but we're being followed.*"

I stopped short.

"*No, keep walking. Act normal. I'm trying to get a scent of who it might be.*"

While Atlas nonchalantly sniffed the air, I reached out with my extra senses, trying to pick up on some small crumb of information. I thought I caught a trace of something dark and thick, but then it was gone, like a small plume of smoke that dissipates as soon as it hits open air. Nothing now. I was sensing nothing. Who was behind us?

And how many times did I need to be followed down a dark street before I would start to be more cautious? Sheesh. *Come on, Dahlia!*

"*When I give the word,*" Atlas said, "*turn around.*"

"*And then what?*"

"*And then get ready to run or fight, I guess. But at least we'll know who's behind us.*"

My mind raced through the possibilities, not only of who it might be but why. Had word gotten out that I was helping to investigate the murder? Could the person responsible be watching my every move? How long had they followed me? Could they be worried I might find the truth? Could I be next on their list?

We turned a corner, and Atlas told me to hide up against the wall of the building. *"Wait until they're close, then we might be able to get a look."*

"And you'll fight them for me if you have to?" I asked.

"Only if I have to. But I'd prefer to run away if that's an option."

I nodded. *"I can get on board with that."*

I heard the footsteps approaching, just on the other side of the corner. The person, whoever it was, was rather stealthy. They made hardly any sound at all, and had it not been for Atlas's exceptional hearing, my thoughts would have remained loud enough inside my head to keep me from ever noticing that I had a tail.

Atlas dropped to a crouch. *"Ready? Now!"*

We both jumped out from behind the corner to surprise the stalker.

I gasped.

Jaymes Hardy yelped in surprise.

"What?" I said, confused.

"Huh?" he replied.

"Why are you following me?"

"I'm... Uh. I'm not."

"Yes, you were."

"No," he insisted. "I'm just on my way..."

I crossed my arms. "On your way where?"

He looked around. "Actually, I must've spaced out. I meant to be heading home. Took a wrong turn. See you, Dahlia." His eyes dropped to Atlas and he swallowed visibly. "Good boy."

He backed away a few steps and then turned and hurried off in the other direction.

I watched him leave. "That's a lot of spacing out to end up all the way over here when he lives in the Outskirts."

Atlas kept his hackles up. I couldn't blame him. This was certainly a night full of strange behavior. Strange and suspicious behavior.

Chapter Thirteen

I received the message from Sheriff Bloom while I was already at Time to Kiln for my shift. Jude was in the studio with a small class of about half a dozen students when I sidled up to him, whispered where I needed to go, and asked if that would be all right.

The werewolf's eyes grew large. "Yes, of course! If Sheriff Bloom needs to speak with you, you go speak with her. Any time. Just lock the door and flip the sign to *closed.*"

So much for being subtle about it. The students were clearly interested in what was going on, and I could almost guarantee they'd be speculating about it as soon as I left.

But when I remembered how good it felt to share a little lighthearted speculation with friends, I started to feel better about it. They would have a good time as they threw, and it likely wouldn't make the investigation any trickier than it already was.

Maybe one day soon, I could be in their position, merely theorizing on things, taking wild guesses and concocting conspiracies, rather than being involved in the situation personally. It sounded lovely.

Atlas accompanied me, and maybe I was mistaken, but it seemed like Jingo greeted us with a shade less suspicion than before when we entered the sheriff's department. Maybe we were starting to earn his trust. Or maybe his attention was simply absorbed by the cross-word puzzle in front of him. He looked up, saw it was us, and said, "She's in her office. Knock first."

I hadn't ever been to Sheriff Bloom's office, but the place wasn't huge, so I kept an eye out as I passed the front desk and found her name on one of the doors without much trouble. I knocked twice.

"Come on in, Dahlia."

Her office looked like a fortress of paperwork inside. Stacks and stacks of parchment filled almost every inch of it, with the exception of a narrow path around the side of her desk and a small break in the stacks for her to peer through.

"Have a seat," she said, flicking her wrist and sending a pile of rolled parchment flying off the chair across from her at the desk. It knocked into a precarious stack and the whole thing collapsed. She didn't seem to care. "Atlas might have to stay standing. Apologies for the cramped space."

"It's fine," I said. "What is all this stuff?"

She sighed and set down the pen she'd been scribbling with. "Reports. The High Council insists that every small thing be logged, every interaction, every interview, every time we sneeze, essentially. 'Utmost accountability' is the policy. Of course, what that translates to in real life is that my office perpetually looks like this, and not a single person on the High Council ever actually reviews a single piece of the paperwork. I could be writing confessions to high crimes on each of these and no one would ever find out because I'm the last person to see any of this."

"But you have to do it?" I asked.

"If I want to follow the rules and guidelines, yes. To be clear, I don't mind accountability. I think a sheriff's department *should* be accountable for the power it holds. But this? This doesn't do anything but keep me locked in my office. I suspect that was the purpose from the start."

"You don't get along with the High Council?"

She smiled. "I do my best. But some people don't appreciate my ability to spot a lie. Strange how it's usually politicians who detest that gift in others..." She grabbed the paper from in front of her, set it on top of one of the teetering stacks, and then clasped her hands together on her desk. "Town politics isn't why I asked you to come see me today. I wanted to talk to you about the Delphelius Twench case. Deputy Manchester has recommended to me that we close the portal to Avalon. I'm inclined to agree with him, but as you can imagine, the paperwork that goes along with something like that is monumental. And I won't exactly be currying any favor with the High Council when I ask for it. So, I thought I'd see if you had anything that could help convince me one way or the other."

"Anything like?"

"New information. Manchester says he'd made you his eyes, ears, and emotions out there."

It was a surreal experience to sit across from the sheriff herself as she asked me for help. Truth be told, I felt quite starstruck being this near to her. She had a presence that seemed too big for Eastwind, though she never did anything to give the impression that she felt above the townsfolk. She just *was* bigger than the rest of us, more powerful, and not just because of her powers or rank. There was a confidence about her that ran deep. The fact that she could spot a lie from a mile away also left one feeling small and humble in her presence.

"Does that mean you've ruled out Naomi Twench?" I asked.

"Haven't ruled her out, but it's not looking promising."

"I... I don't think it was her. I think it was somebody else."

Bloom's brows rose. "And who do you think it was?"

"I don't know precisely. Deputy Manchester said it was almost impossible to narrow the suspect pool, so I haven't been focusing on that. Instead, I've been trying to find people who jump out to me for one reason or another."

"And?"

"It's only a preliminary list, I suppose, but two other people stand out. And I had this feeling... No, never mind that."

The sheriff leaned forward. "No, no, let's absolutely mind that. What was the feeling?"

"It was... I think Nora called it Insight."

"Ooh, yes, Ruby True has that as well. A useful Fifth Wind trait. And what was your Insight telling you?"

"Last night it was telling me that I'd encountered the killer at some point throughout my day. But I hadn't seen Naomi Twench at all."

"Interesting. That's why you feel like you can rule her out." She shrugged. "For what it's worth, she hasn't said much, but in my brief time with her, I didn't get the sense that she'd killed her husband. I think she was too connected to him—or perhaps chained to him is a better description—to even consider the idea."

"Did Deputy Manchester tell you what she said to me? That she was glad someone had done it?"

Bloom nodded. "I'm inclined to believe her on that. I think she's glad it happened, but that doesn't change the fact that I don't think she could've imagined killing him as an option. They'd been together so long. Sometimes people become linked like that. It's not healthy for either one, but it's like they've started to swap parts, blending into each other. They'd just as soon kill themself as they would the other person. No, I don't think she had it in her, despite the fact that she yelled at him and said some hurtful things right before he died. So perhaps we can both agree to move on from her as a suspect, at least until we have a reason to circle back. You said there were others acting strangely. Who might that be?"

"One of them is named Lifton. I don't know his last name. He's a tour guide from Avalon, but it sounds like he knew Echo Chambers from a while back."

"Ah yes, Lifton Heits. I remember that name from Deputy Culpepper's report. A witch from Avalon, if I remember correctly. He was at Sheehan's Pub that night."

"It was more than just being there," I said. "He was outside when it happened." I explained how I'd run into him while I was following Delphelius's ghost out to the body.

"And what would be the motive?" asked Bloom.

"It might sound shaky, but I wonder if he thought it would improve the experience of his tour group. I followed him around last night, and you wouldn't believe the stories he was making up about the town. He doesn't seem to know a thing about the place, or if he does, he ignores it. He was making up morbid stories left and right. Some werewolf attacked a woman here, an elf jumped to her death from the clock tower—total fabrications."

"Well, that last thing *did* happen a while back. But I see your point. You think he might've killed Delphelius to create a certain image of Eastwind that might drive more people to want to visit and might encourage the tourists to tell their friends about his service?"

I stared down at my hands folded in my lap. "When you say it like that, it does sound like a thin motive."

"People have killed for less, I assure you."

"There *is* one other thing about him. Remember how I said he seemed to know Echo? Is it possible that he might've, I dunno, lived in Eastwind when he was younger? Maybe even have gone to Mancer Academy?"

Bloom arched a brow. "Go on."

"Raven Goode said she kept thinking she recognized the tourists, but she couldn't have, because they're all Avalonian. But what if one of them isn't? And what if it's Lifton? He looks to be around her age. Maybe he went by something different while he lived here."

"Hmm..." said Bloom. "They do offer plenty of services in Avalon to change the way you look. That's an interesting theory. Do you suppose that might mean there's an additional motive that could exist? Perhaps Delphelius and Lifton knew each other in their younger years?"

"Maybe. And from speaking to Delphelius, it sounds like he was the kind of person to make enemies in those days."

"Oh, most certainly," she said. "I can confirm that. Mancer Academy prefers to handle all its disciplinary matters on its own, and I'm mostly fine with that, but every now and then something happens that's too big for them to manage, and they judge that it's time for our department to get involved. That was the case with some of Delphelius's antics. Not once, but twice I was called in to handle a situation. I believe the first time was when he blasted another student's ear off, and the second time was when he cast a spell that nearly drowned another student—I managed to get a hold of Ruby, who helped us, um, *resuscitate* the child." Her face made it clear that she'd chosen the word "resuscitate" carefully.

I understood what she really meant, though. She'd called in a favor that only Ruby could do and broken one of the taboos that Fifth Winds carried around. That student hadn't *nearly* drowned at all. They'd *drowned* drowned. Fully. To the point where only a necromancer could undo it. I'd done the same thing to those mice and the snake in the studio only a few months before, so I got the gist of it.

"If Delphelius and Lifton knew each other back then," I continued, "maybe there was a longstanding grudge."

Bloom tapped a finger to her chin. "Very interesting. I don't remember there being anyone named Lifton Heits in town, but name changes happen. There's a possible problem with the means, but we can circle back to that in a moment. Who else do you have your eye on?"

I hesitated. It was one thing to suspect someone based on a feeling, but another thing entirely to direct the sheriff's attention their way in a murder investigation.

"I'm not totally set on this one, but there's something strange going on with Jaymes Hardy."

Bloom chuckled dryly. "I'm sure there is. There's usually something strange going on with a Hardy. I don't know Jaymes particularly well, though, so tell me more."

"He was at Sheehan's the night of the murder."

"So were a lot of people," she countered.

"He came inside right *after* Delphelius walked out to relieve himself in the alley."

Bloom half-smiled. "Is *that* what he was doing back there?"

"Apparently so. He told me the bathroom was occupied, so he went into the alley. There was an overlap of time between when he went into the alley and when Jaymes walked into the pub. Jaymes might've been outside already, chatting with one of the werewolves he knows from the compound."

"And what possible motive would Jaymes have for killing Delphelius?"

I hesitated. This theory was a bit slapdash, but the pieces could fit together if I made them. "Jaymes has been poking around the necromancy section at the Pixie Mixie."

Bloom narrowed her eyes at me. "Strange thing for a werewolf to do. Go on."

"Well, it got me thinking, because like you said, it's a strange thing for a werewolf to do. But what if he's not fully werewolf? I asked Jane Saxon about it, and she said she didn't know who his father was. Could be a werewolf, but it could also be a witch."

"Ah."

"I don't know why that would lead Jaymes to the necromancy section, but it does make sense as to why he might think he was capable of spell magic at all. Only, who would his father be?"

"You have a guess," she said.

"The pieces might just fit."

Bloom nodded. "I wouldn't put it past Delphelius to step out on his wife like that. But even if we could determine that he was Jaymes's father, what motive would Jaymes have for murder?"

"That's where I draw a blank. Maybe he's upset that his father didn't stick around? Didn't help out? But Jaymes did have the opportunity to commit the murder. Also, and this might be nothing, but he was following me around Eastwind last night."

That caught Bloom's attention. "Following you?"

"Atlas was with me, but yes. Jaymes was following us and trying not to let us know. When I caught him, he said he had spaced out and taken a wrong turn on his way home."

"Lost on his way to the Scandrick compound?"

"Exactly," I replied, understanding her confusion. "And no, I wasn't heading that direction."

"Your theory of why he was tailing you is what?"

I shrugged. "Maybe he knows that I'm investigating the murder and wants to figure out what I know."

A crease appeared above her nose. "Or he wants to make sure whatever you know doesn't get out." She paused, her gaze drifting up toward the ceiling. "You know, I briefly encountered Jaymes about a year ago. His mother died, and we were called out to the compound. Someone thought it was suspicious and sent an anonymous tip our way. I always suspected it was Jaymes who sent the message, but I never could confirm it."

"And did her death look suspicious?" I asked.

"In some ways, yes. For one, she was a fairly healthy werewolf in her mid-forties. It didn't make sense that she would simply not wake up one morning. But that does sometimes happen. People die of natural causes."

"Did the medical examiner find anything?"

"No, because we weren't given permission to take the body with us. So neither the medical examiner nor the magical examiner ever got to take a look. Jaymes was distraught. Hardly spoke to anyone while we were there, just sat in the corner of his mother's bedroom and stared at her bed."

"What if he was right?" I said. "What if there was foul play? What if he suspected Delphelius had something to do with it?"

"And he took it upon himself to exact revenge? Possible." She paused, considered it, then shook her head. "It's unlikely, though. The means is where it goes awry." She opened a desk drawer, rifled through the contents, and then pulled out a slip of parchment. "This is the magical examiner's preliminary report for Delphelius."

She spun the document around so it was right-side up for me, but I didn't understand what any of it meant. Thankfully, she explained.

"The medical examiner hasn't concluded her inspection of his body yet, but already there's something that interests me from the magical examiner's office." She pointed to a particular phrase, and I leaned over to read the handwriting. It seemed medical professionals in every realm struggled with writing legibly.

Finally, I decoded the words. "Signs of pyromancy?" I looked up at Sheriff Bloom, who nodded.

"We'll have to wait to open up Delphelius to see what the damage is—gruesome, I apologize—but for now, we know that the magical examiner detected signs of pyromancy on the body immediately before death."

"And that couldn't be from Delphelius himself, right? Can East Wind witches cast pyromancy?"

"Not generally. Maybe a little bit here and there, but most give up on trying by the time they're his age and lean into their natural abilities to get the job done."

"Does that mean you think a South Wind did it?" I asked. The South Winds were the witches who had literal fire power.

Sheriff Bloom slid the report back toward her and then placed it on top of one of the precarious stacks by her chair. "We'll need to figure out if the pyromancy was what ultimately killed him, but that's my top lead, since we have nothing else to go on."

"Then that would rule out Naomi Twench, right?" I asked.

"If the assumption that pyromancy was the cause of death is correct, then I believe it does. I've never seen an elf wield fire as a weapon in all my years."

"It doesn't rule out Lifton Heits," I said.

"It doesn't rule out *anyone*," Sheriff Bloom corrected me, "because we don't officially know that it's the cause of death."

"Oh, right."

"But I know what you mean. Go on, what were you about to say about Lifton?"

"We know he's a witch, because I heard Echo mention it, but I don't know what kind of witch he is."

Bloom nodded. "We should probably find that out."

"And what about Jaymes? Let's say Delphelius is his father and Jaymes inherited some of the powers. Delphelius was an East Wind witch, so does that mean Jaymes would also have hydromancy powers? Or could he have pyromancy instead?"

"Two witches will give birth to a witch, but the Wind that the child can harness is unknown until they enter their school years and begin to dive into their powers. I assume the same could be true for a werewolf who inherits some witching powers. Even if Jaymes's father isn't a South Wind specifically, Jaymes could, technically, end up with some traces of South Wind magic."

"That doesn't help us much, then."

"No, but we now understand the steps for moving forward. In the meantime, allow me to return to my initial question: do you believe we should close the portal to Avalon?"

I couldn't believe she was asking *me* an important question like that. "I don't know. Maybe I've missed something completely here."

"Maybe we all have."

"Would you rather be safe than sorry?" I asked.

"If I close the portal I'll be safe *and* sorry, thanks to the grief I'll no doubt receive from the High Council. But if I don't close the portal I might be unsafe and also sorry." She sighed. "Okay. I'll ask them to close it for a day to get us started. In the meantime, I would greatly appreciate it if you could continue to help out with the investigation. I would have Deputy Manchester or Culpepper go speak with Jaymes and Lifton, but it sounds like both suspects are more likely to open up to you. And also, Fritta Ashpot just caused a cauldron explosion in Copperstone Heights, and Manchester will likely be wrapped up with that nonsense for the rest of the day. Keep your hellhound close by, though, because I don't trust either of those suspects at this point."

I nodded. "I need to get back to the studio, but after my shift—"

Bloom held up a hand. "All due respect, this investigation is slightly more important than making sure people can buy a new scrying bowl at a moment's notice. I'll send a message to Raven and Jude to let them know I need you for the rest of the day, at least. And here." She reached into another drawer and pulled out a small coin purse, which she slid across the almost nonexistent open space on her desk. "Take this for any expenses. Treating yourself and Atlas to meals is considered an expense, by the way. I don't need any of that back. We have a small discretionary fund that we never get around to spending."

I grabbed the coin purse. It was heavier than I'd expected. Wow, was I being paid for a job again? This was starting to seem way more lucrative than working at the studio, albeit with less predictable hours.

Oh, and it was much more dangerous...

Chapter Fourteen

Atlas was more than happy to accompany me to Medium Rare. While I wasn't there for a meal in particular, I couldn't ignore the coin purse weighing heavily in my pocket. Might as well grab something for both of us while we were there—it was nearly lunchtime anyway. And it would be nice to insist that Nora charge me full price for once.

Lifton and his group of tourists weren't at Medium Rare. The odds of running into them were slim, but a girl could dream. I wanted to get this all sorted out by the end of the day, if possible, so Sheriff Bloom wouldn't have to extend the portal closure any longer than necessary.

The diner was busy, but thankfully, no crowd was waiting outside when I arrived. Maybe the tourists were starting to thin out. Maybe Nora would finally get more than a few hours of sleep at a time.

The bell above the door chimed as Atlas and I stepped inside. I glanced around and waved at Ted, who had his usual corner booth to himself. Mudbug, his ghost cat, was perched on the seat next to him. Nora didn't usually allow animals on the furniture, but she made an exception for ghost animals, and I was glad she did. Mudbug had her head resting on Ted's lap, and even though she had no physical form, Ted stroked her head lovingly as he sipped his coffee. I liked to believe that on some level, Mudbug could feel the gentle caresses of the reaper's gloved hand.

At the far end of the dining room, I spotted Jaymes talking to a table of werewolves. Hendrix Hardy was among them, so I assumed the others were from the Scandrick compound as well. Not that it mattered to me —I wasn't here to chat with them. I was here for Jaymes.

I found an open seat at the counter and slid in, while Atlas wandered over to Ted's table to join the begging party Grim had already started.

Nora approached me first, sliding a glass of water and a coffee mug in front of me. "I thought you were working at the studio today."

"I thought so too. Sheriff Bloom had other ideas."

"Ah. Better you than me." She pulled out her order pad. "Burger and fries?"

"Sounds good. And I'm paying today."

"No, you're not."

"Yes, I am. Bloom gave me discretionary money since I'm helping out."

She nodded once. "Then yes, you are paying. And you'd better tip well."

I laughed. "That depends on the service. Speaking of which, would you mind assigning Jaymes to this seat?"

Nora appeared confused, but only for a moment before her understanding clicked into place. "Oh. Yes, sure. That's interesting. Okay." I could tell she was torn between asking for more information and staying the heck out of it. She opted for staying the heck out of it and tucked her order pad away without writing anything down. "Jaymes," she hollered at him, "when you get a minute?" and then she pointed at me.

When Jaymes saw who she was pointing to, he nearly sprinted over, forgetting all about the werewolves he'd been chatting with. "Hi, Dahlia! Hey, so, um, about last night. I was thinking about it, and I realize that you probably think I'm a total creep and that I was following you or something. I promise that wasn't the case. I just get lost in my head sometimes. I was up at Whirligig's Garden Center, getting a few tomato plants for the compound—ours didn't do so well last year, so we wanted to try a new variety—and I just started wandering around on my way home, totally lost in my head."

"I believe you," I said, deciding not to point out that I hadn't seen any such tomato plants in his arms.

"You do?"

"Yeah, totally. The same thing happens to me some-times. I get to thinking about something, and everything else slips away. I give a whole new meaning to 'lost in my thoughts.' I found myself out by the Parchment Catacombs last week when I'd meant to head over to Ezra's Outfitters for a new amulet." I was surprised by how easily the lie lent itself to me. Was that a sign that I wasn't as good of a person as I liked to believe, or was it a sign that I was becoming a better sleuth? Maybe both.

Jaymes's relief was easily visible. His shoulders dropped. "Oh good. Yeah, I was just thinking about it again, and I figured you probably thought I was some creep following you. I don't want to follow you. Or anyone. I just... Yeah."

He stared at me unblinkingly until I grew seriously uncomfortable and said, "I think I'm ready to order."

"Right! Right." He pulled out an order pad from his back pocket. "Okay, what can I get you?"

I ordered the burger and fries. "And be sure to charge me," I added. "I know Nora says not to, but I have some money and I want to pay."

"Not on my watch." He grinned. "If she makes you pay, I'll just put it on my tab."

"No, really," I said, wondering why he was suddenly offering to cover my bill; we weren't necessarily friends, after all. "I want to pay."

He left to turn in the ticket without another word about it, and I suspected he had no intention of offering me a tab to pay.

Nora came by a few minutes later to refill my coffee mug. She was carrying a full one with her, too.

"Okay, fine. You win. I can't stay away. What's going on with Jaymes? Anything I need to know about?" She took a sip from her drink and set it on the counter between us.

"Do you really want to know? I don't want to drag you into this if you're busy."

"Of course I want to know," she snapped. "I *always* want to know. I have a problem. I can't stay away, even when I'm up to my ears in tourists." I could tell her annoyance was more at herself than at me, so I didn't let it bother me.

"Fair enough." I filled her in on what I knew about Jaymes, including our encounter the night before.

Her eyes followed him over the rim of her coffee mug. "Okay, maybe Jane was right. Maybe I shouldn't have hired him. I knew he was a little weird, but so is everyone in this town. I thought he was the usual kind of strange. Maybe even the fun kind."

"I don't know yet that he's done anything," I reminded her. "But I do want to find out a little bit more about him. Specifically, I want to know if he knows who his father is."

"Delphelius makes a certain kind of sense," Nora replied. "My only question is when he might've had the time between making Naomi's life miserable and drinking at Sheehan's to meet Jaymes's mother and, ya know."

The bell rang behind Nora, and she looked over her shoulder at the open window to the kitchen. "That's your order. I better make myself look busy so Jaymes can bring it over and you can ask him what you need."

When Jaymes set down the plate in front of me, he lingered. While a little uncomfortable, it was also what I'd hoped for. "This is perfect," I said. "I'm so hungry. The sheriff has me working this case with Delphelius on top of my usual job."

I knew it was a risky thing to let a suspect know, but I wanted to see his reaction, possibly even get a read on his emotions, if they were strong enough to stand out among the mélange in the diner.

I certainly sensed a wave of eagerness coming from him. Interesting. He stared at me through wide, dark eyes. "You're working the case?"

"Sort of. As much as someone who isn't technically law enforcement can. I'm helping out."

His gaze remained startlingly fixed to me as he said, "Is that because you can speak with Delphelius's ghost?"

I nodded and took the first bite of my burger.

"Did he tell you who killed him, then?"

I was in dangerous territory now. Jaymes's eagerness increased, and if he were the killer, confirming that Delphelius had given me that information—which he obviously hadn't, or else I'd be done with this mess— would make me a target. "Unfortunately, no," I said around the wad of burger in my mouth. He waited attentively for me to finish chewing, and I used the opportunity to try to come up with the best approach. "Delphelius isn't very useful," I continued. "I think that's what his wife was so mad about when she chewed him out, actually."

"I heard about that," he said, "but I didn't see it. What was she mad about?"

"She said he was as good to her dead as he was alive. Basically calling him a waste of space. He said he'd help out at their home, and instead he was in the pub again. Sounds like a pretty irresponsible person."

I tried to reach out and feel around for Jaymes's reaction to that, but I didn't find anything different. "But you did speak with him, right? That's a thing you can do with necromancy?" he asked.

I popped a fry into my mouth. "Yeah, it is. If you're a Fifth Wind. But I don't know that anyone else could pull off that level of necromancy, outside of, say, Ted. And why would they want to?"

Jaymes appeared suddenly less interested. "I dunno. Maybe they have a ghost they want to speak with. If it could help solve a murder, I can see why a person would want the ability."

"Hey," I said, casually dunking a fry into the small ramekin of ketchup, "you didn't know Delphelius, did you?"

"Not really. I saw him around the pub sometimes. I heard he was a pain in the hide."

"I'm definitely gathering that from speaking to people. And, frankly, from speaking to Delphelius himself."

Jaymes cracked a smile. "How's the burger?"

"Delicious."

"I'll let you get to it, then. Good luck on the investigation."

And then he walked away, leaving me with very little new information to go on. From his responses, there was definitely something happening. He was especially interested in whether or not I could speak with Delphelius personally, but I hadn't sensed any anxiety about it from him, only a strange enthusiasm. What was that about?

Nora came back over a few minutes later, taking a sip from her coffee mug that she'd left on the counter in front of me. "Anything?"

"I don't know. He's really interested in the fact that I could speak with Delphelius's ghost."

Nora gave me a knowing look. "Certainly something of interest, yeah?"

"I thought so, but we already know that he's overly interested in necro—" I cut myself off as Jaymes rounded the counter, walking toward Nora.

"Hey," he said, "can you tell me if there's any cherry pie in the case down there, or is it only apple left?" He pointed down the counter to the two pie displays, and both Nora and I leaned over to get a better look. The glass coverings distorted the contents enough that it was difficult to make out from this angle.

"Looks like we have both," Nora concluded.

"Oh great, thanks. Table twelve was thinking about dessert, and I didn't want to offer them anything we didn't have."

"Good thinking," Nora said flatly, clearly not impressed by him doing the very basics of his job.

Jaymes wandered away, and she turned back to me. "You're right, we do already know he's into necromancy, but that doesn't mean he killed Delphelius. Did you ask if he knew who his dad was?"

I nearly rolled my eyes at her. "How would I bring that up? That's not exactly small talk."

"Neither is a murder investigation."

"True." In the moment's pause, we both grabbed our coffee mugs to drink. Before mine could touch my lips, I heard a deep, rattling voice command, "Don't drink that!"

I froze and looked around. Ted was standing up in the corner booth, waving his scythe in the air. His voice had sent a chill over the diner, which was now deathly silent. He repeated himself. "Don't drink that."

Nora held up her mug. "This?"

"Yes! Don't drink the coffee. Either of you."

Nora and I set down our mugs. "Why?" she asked.

Ted pointed a long, gloved finger directly at Jaymes. "Because he just slipped something in your drinks."

Jaymes's eyes went wide. The werewolf looked more like a deer in the headlights. For a moment, nobody seemed to breathe.

Then Jaymes tossed away the menus in his hands and took off for the door.

"Oh no you don't," Nora yelled, stripping off her apron and running around the counter to pursue him out the door. I figured I'd better not leave her hanging, so I jumped up from my seat and followed.

Jaymes wasn't heading directly toward the Dead-woods, which was lucky. But he was definitely heading somewhere, sprinting with the speed reserved for a young man in his prime with a guilty conscience.

I was not built for running. Never had been. I had no speed at all, and I was terribly out of shape. My lungs were already burning and I was hardly twenty yards outside the diner. Nora seemed to have slightly more stamina, or perhaps she had more ready access to her outrage and that was fueling her, but even she wasn't closing the distance. He was only getting farther and farther ahead of us.

The Scandrick compound, I thought. Of course. That's where he was heading. We wouldn't be allowed in, and once he was through those gates, we might not see him for weeks, if not years. I'd heard that some people spent their whole lives without leaving the compound, so it was possible that this would be the last we'd see of him, if we didn't find a way to catch him. And it looked like we wouldn't.

Then suddenly two large beasts raced past me.

The speed with which both Atlas and Grim could move was alarming. They closed the gap quickly, and Atlas was the first to reach Jaymes, running straight into him and knocking the werewolf face-first into a heap on the ground. He rolled and cursed, and before he could come to a complete stop, Grim had him pinned down.

I tried to jog over, but a side stitch made me limp. By the time I'd made it to Jaymes, Nora was already drilling him with questions between her sharp intakes of air.

Grim had made way for her to roll Jaymes over onto his back, and she had the collar of his shirt gripped in her fist. "What in the hellhound did you put in our drinks?"

Jaymes looked terrified and wouldn't tear his eyes away from Grim's exposed fangs.

"It wasn't going to hurt you," he insisted.

Nora shook him. "What was it?"

I clasped my hands together on top of my head, trying to look fierce but desperate to get rid of the shard of pain in my side. Atlas and Grim stood on either side of Jaymes, locked on to him. If he tried to run, he wouldn't get far.

"It was just a little bit of dried dragon's blood. From the Pixie Mixie. Not even in the restricted back room. Just readily available stuff."

"What was that for?"

"I just..." He looked like he was about to cry, and I could feel the emotions welling up in him.

"He's too scared," I said between gasping breaths. "Give him a little bit of space to think. If he tries to run, Grim and Atlas will catch him."

Nora hesitated before letting go of his shirt and taking a step back. Jaymes remained on his back on the mulchy ground and covered his eyes with a forearm. If he thought we wouldn't know he was on the verge of tears, he was wrong. "I just wanted some of your powers. That's all. Just a little. I wouldn't take them all."

Nora scowled down at him. "You can't have our powers, numbskull. You're a werewolf."

"I'm not completely a werewolf," he moaned. "My father was a witch."

"Delphelius?" I asked.

"Huh?" He removed his arm from his eyes and stared up at me, befuddled.

"Was Delphelius your father?"

"No! Ugh. No, my father was named Portridge. He was a West Wind. Died only a year after I was born, but never had anything to do with me or my mother. You thought Delphelius was my father?"

Embarrassment crept into my face. "No. But you can see why I had to ask."

He sat up. "You thought I killed Delphelius, didn't you?"

"I didn't know! You showed up at the pub right after he—"

Nora stepped forward. "We're asking the questions here, kid. You just answer them. Why were you trying to steal our powers?"

Jaymes flopped onto his back again. "I wanted to see if I could speak with my mother. She died a year ago, and I've wondered if it was accidental like everyone said. I was told she gathered the wrong mushrooms from the forest and ate them and then didn't wake up, but my mother wouldn't do that. She'd been gathering mushrooms her whole life. The kind they said she ate didn't even look like edible ones."

"You think she was murdered?" I asked.

He nodded miserably. "No one in the compound will listen to me. I thought that maybe if I could summon her spirit, I could ask her. Get some closure. And then I saw that there was a job open at Medium Rare, and it just seemed like fate, like maybe I was meant to be near a Fifth Wind to tap into those powers. Then you came around, Dahlia, and it just... I thought maybe if I could tap some powers from both of you, I wouldn't have to take as much from either one, and I could still have enough to talk to my mom."

"Is this why you were following me around town?" I asked.

He nodded. "I'm sorry. I realize how much of a creep it makes me. But I wanted to get to know you better. I thought if I could do that, I could make you my friend and it would be easier to convince you..." His voice trailed off.

Nora sighed exasperatedly. "Stalking people isn't how you make friends, Jaymes."

She and I shared a begrudging look of understanding. Tough to get mad at someone who was just trying to get to the truth about his mother.

"For fang's sake," Nora said, leaning over and offering him a hand to pull him to his feet. "You could've just asked. I wouldn't have given you any powers, but I could help you try to summon your mother if her spirit isn't already out of reach."

He blinked at her. "Really? You would do that?"

"Of course."

Jaymes groaned. "That never occurred to me. Sorry. No one in the compound has ever believed me, so I figured everyone out here would think I was crazy, too."

"I'm not saying I *don't* think you're crazy," Nora said, making it clear she wasn't in a better mood, even if she did believe his excuse for spiking our coffees.

"But you'll help me?"

"If I can. And when I'm not swamped at the diner, which I'm about to be again, because you're definitely fired."

Jaymes's eyes went wide. "What?"

"You're fired," she said. "I can't have someone working for me who tampers with drinks."

He dropped his head. "Okay, fair enough. Are you also going to turn me into the deputies, too?"

"Nah, they have enough going on right now. Go home, Jaymes. I'll let you know when I can help with your mother."

He turned and slumped toward the compound. We watched him go.

"I really want to tackle him again," Atlas said.

Grim, meanwhile, moaned, *"I think I'm more out of shape than I realized,"* and proceeded to vomit into a small shrub.

Chapter Fifteen

If I could've hopped on Atlas and ridden him like Monty liked to do, I would've. My legs felt like Jell-O from my brief sprint after Jaymes, but I had to walk across town anyway. I needed to find Lifton Heits. I needed to make sure he wouldn't try to murder someone else before the end of his stay in Eastwind. Unless we'd missed something obvious, he was the last viable suspect.

Thanks to the nuisance the tourist groups were making of themselves in Eastwind, it only took a little asking around once Atlas and I had made it to the Emporium to figure out where Lifton and his group had headed. It was Mershali, one of the fruit vendors, who helped us. "They're heading to the cemetery. They wouldn't shut up about it. They want to see if they can communicate with any spirits." He'd rolled his eyes. "Do they not have spirits in Avalon? I mean, come on. Let the dead rest, for fang's sake."

I'd thanked him for the information and made for the cemetery.

The Eastwind Cemetery wasn't somewhere I'd had a desire to visit before. I'd been to plenty of graveyards and such back in New Orleans—I even walked by one almost every day on my way to the wealthier neighborhood that could afford my cleaning services—and it'd never bothered me. But I wasn't a Fifth Wind back then. Now I was.

It wasn't that the Eastwind Cemetery scared me. It was more that I'd heard it was a playground for restless spirits that didn't care to move on, whose unfinished business was much more mundane than solving their own murder and would therefore likely never be resolved. In the cemetery, they could converse with each other and be themselves, unseen by almost everyone in town. Except for me. Going there felt like I might be intruding.

But if Lifton was there, I had to go. I was pretty sure Naomi wasn't responsible for her husband's death, since it seemed that pyromancy might play a part, and while Jaymes had certainly been acting suspicious, that was well explained by his desire to find the truth about his deceased mother. That left one suspect: Lifton Heits.

And if he wasn't the one, then... we were in trouble. We'd have to start from square one, reinvestigating everyone who was outside during the window of when Delphelius was murdered.

The cemetery was atop a hill not far from Fluke

Mountain, on the outer edge of town. I spied the group almost immediately and decided to take the long way around to the back side of the land, where I could remain somewhat hidden among a sprinkling of ancient trees.

"Do you want me to come with you?" Atlas asked. *"I don't exactly hide well."*

It was true. His white coat and large size made him easy enough to notice. Surely Lifton would catch on if he saw us following him again.

But I did want Atlas with me. His courage tended to be bigger than his fear when it counted. "There," I said, pointing to a muddy spot on the ground. "Just this once, maybe you could roll—"

The wild animal in him took over before I could finish my sentence. He rolled and flopped in the mud until almost none of his white coat was visible through the grunge. He'd done the job well, and I frowned down at him. "We'll probably have to wash you down outside tonight. I don't think Nora and Tanner would appreciate you bringing that into the house." I sighed. "But you did well, Atlas. Let's go."

We walked around the perimeter of the cemetery to the back gate, where we let ourselves in. They had locked up the cemeteries and graveyards in New Orleans to keep people out, but it didn't look like the thought had occurred to them in Eastwind. Mostly, people didn't want to come mess around here. It wasn't a question of "are there ghosts?" but rather, "will the ghosts come after me?"

I reminded Atlas to watch where he walked so as not to tread over someone's grave, and then the two of us crept as close as we could to the tourists without being seen.

"You have better hearing than I do," I said. *"We need to know if Lifton is a South Wind witch. If you hear anything that makes you suspect he is, let me know."*

A large crypt provided convenient shelter to hide behind that allowed us to get closer to the group, easily within earshot. It helped that they slowly made their way closer as Lifton pointed to one grave then another, reciting stories that I had no doubt were complete fabrications.

"Oh, Lilith Abernathy," he declared. "Hers is a story for the books! She was murdered by two werewolves on her way to the Emporium. They snuck up on her and pounced, for no other reason than sport."

A woman's spirit appeared beside me, causing me to clasp a hand over my mouth to keep from yelping at the shock and giving away my hiding place.

"That never happened," she said. "I died from falling off my roof when I was repairing the thatching." She stepped out from behind the crypt and braced her hands on her hips as she stared straight at Lifton and demanded, "Who in the Sphinx's riddle are you, and why are you making up lies about me?"

But he couldn't hear or see her, so she didn't get the answer she wanted. She gave up and vanished as he continued to lead the avid listeners along a stone path between the graves.

They came close enough that I turned to Atlas. *"We'd better move so they don't see us here."*

We tiptoed away and found a long shadow cast by the afternoon sun from one of the ancient trees throughout the property. The only problem was that now we were too far away for me to hear the conversation.

I tried to creep closer without giving away my hiding place, but I stopped when I nearly stepped carelessly into an open grave. "Oh shoot!" I caught myself before I fell. The shadow on the ground had nearly obscured the hole. Not the place I would want to find myself. I walked around to stand at the end of the long rectangular ditch, and found that while the grave was empty, a headstone had already been placed there, welcoming the future occupant.

It was for Delphelius Twench.

I shivered. It wasn't a terrible resting place for someone, in the shadow of the giant, wise tree. But the hole felt like a gaping mouth, and I couldn't help but remember that Delphelius's body, which hadn't been his spirit's home for days now, was still being poked and prodded by the magical examiner and medical examiner. Had they found anything else of use? Some clue that would confirm who it was that had taken Delphelius's life in that alley beside the pub?

Perhaps my thoughts had conjured him, but Delphelius's spirit appeared at the bottom of the hole. He stared up at me, bemused. "Still haven't figured it out yet?"

"I'm working on it. It's not like you're being much help."

"Oh sure," he said, "blame me. I'm only the *victim* of this whole thing, in case you forgot."

I did feel a little bad for getting frustrated with him. "Sorry," I said. "This isn't easy."

"You know what else isn't easy? Being a ghost. Being dead. Never getting to have another beer for all eternity. You think I give a pile of unicorn swirls how you feel about this investigation? Please. Suck it up. Don't forget that I'm the victim here."

My guilt for being short with him quickly dissipated. "You know I'm only helping with this out of the goodness of my heart, right?"

"Swirls! The sheriff gave you a coin purse."

I gasped. "You're *watching* me?"

"When it's not too boring of a show, sure."

"She only gave me that money to allow me to skip work. I didn't expect anything from her or anyone else when I started."

"Tell yourself whatever you need to feel all high and mighty," said Delphelius. "Won't change the fact that you're a busybody who stinks at sleuthing."

I opened my mouth to respond, but Atlas's low growl stopped me short. I looked at my familiar then realized he was looking at something on the other side of me. I turned quickly and found one of the tourists was standing next to me, staring into the grave. Could he see Delphelius? But then I realized Delphelius had disappeared. The tourist was simply staring into the hypnotizing ditch, as I had been before the spirit appeared.

"Crazy to think we all end up here," said the man. I recognized him as the same one who'd been emptying his stomach outside the pub on the night of the murder.

I felt a sudden sense of danger with him standing next to me, but figured it was a result of having lost myself in my argument with Delphelius to the point where I'd given up my hiding spot to at least one person. The rest of the tourists were still captivated by Lifton's fantastical tales of murder, though. Only this man had noticed me, it seemed, and he had broken from the group to come chat.

I didn't yet want to ask why.

"Do you plan on being buried?" he asked.

It was a strange question, though perhaps an obvious conversation starter in a cemetery. "I haven't thought about it, actually."

"Makes sense. You're still young. I never thought about it when I was your age. Now, though? I'm getting up there in years."

I turned to take a good look at him, to try to guess his age. My brain never got around to that assessment, though, because before I could focus on his wrinkles, another detail stood out to me: he was missing an ear.

My body froze. *"Atlas. He's missing an ear."*

Atlas knew what that meant as instantly as I did.

The pieces were clicking together. My hellhound stalked closer slowly, trying not to scare the man away, but making sure he was close enough... just in case.

I tried to play it cool. "Is this your first visit to Eastwind?"

The man chuckled dryly. "No. No it's not." He turned his attention to the name on the headstone, and the wave of glee that emanated from him all but confirmed my suspicions. I'd felt that glee before. "Ah, Del, you terrible excuse for a witch." He spat into the empty grave. "You thought I'd forget."

I took a small step to the side to add some distance between me and this man.

This killer.

"You knew him?" I asked as innocently as I could.

The man turned and looked at me for a moment before offering his hand. "Kannin Bridgewater."

Unsure what else to do, I said, "Dahlia Wildes," and we shook. "You wouldn't happen to be related to the Bridgewaters who live in Eastwind, would you?" I asked.

He nodded. "Levi Bridgewater is my second cousin."

"Are you here to visit them?"

He slipped his hands into the pockets of his red robes. "No. They don't know I'm in town. We weren't close."

"But you knew Delphelius?"

"Sure did. Went to school with him."

"You're a witch," I said.

He nodded.

"What kind?"

He turned to look at me again. "I thought you'd have already put that together."

A voice inside me told me to run, but my feet didn't seem to get the memo. Atlas's hackles rose, and I could tell it was taking everything in him not to turn tail and sprint off. Only his loyalty was keeping him in place.

"Why did you come over here to speak with me?" I asked.

"Why have you been following us around?" Kannin countered. Before I could answer, he said, "Don't worry. I already know. You're a Fifth Wind. Ruby was the only one around back when I lived here, but she also had a hellhound familiar."

Atlas let out a low growl.

"Not yet," I said.

"I'm not gonna hurt you," Kannin continued. "I don't feel the need. I don't feel much of anything. Haven't for quite a while."

And yet that glee still pulsed from him every time his gaze returned to the headstone. And something else. Relief.

"Did you do it?" I asked, nodding toward the empty grave.

Kannin stared into the hole. "Did I do *what?*"

I had to muster every ounce of bravery inside of me to spell it out, to put together the dreadful words. "Did you murder Delphelius Twench?"

He looked up at me, smirking. "Now why would I do a thing like that?"

He turned, put his back to me, and began walking away.

"Wait!" I called after him, but he didn't stop. He met back up with the rest of the tourists without a second glance over his shoulder at me.

He had said enough for me to understand the basics, but I hadn't gotten anything near a confession from him. And it looked like he had no intention of offering one up. Not to me, at least. But I knew someone who might have better luck.

All I had to do was convince her to confront a killer.

Chapter Sixteen

When I burst through the front door of Time to Kiln, panting because why on earth had I thought I was in shape enough to walk that fast from the cemetery after I'd already chased a kid down today, Sasha Cosmo stared at me wide-eyed from behind the shop desk.

The elf jumped to her feet. "Are you being chased? You know you have a hellhound next to you who could probably fight. Running might not be your thing." She took Atlas in fully, muddy fur and all, and said, "Haven's edge... What happened to you two?"

My pride kept me from bracing myself on my thighs to suck in air. "Is Raven here?"

"I think so. The evening class is starting in an hour."

Forget about the evening class. Jude could cover for her. I had something more important for her to do.

I told Atlas to wait outside for me so he didn't track dirt clods in everywhere, and then entered the studio to find Raven reading a book in the break room, her feet kicked up on the table as she leaned back in the chair.

"Raven!" I said, still panting.

"Bubbling cauldron!" she said, nearly falling out of her chair at my sudden intrusion. She caught herself at the last second, but her socked feet slipped off the table. "What's the matter?"

"I need your help."

"You also need some water, clearly," she said. "Your face is red. Are you overheating? Have a seat."

"There's no time." I still needed to send a letter to the sheriff, and now that Kannin Bridgewater knew I knew, what would he try?

"There's also no time for you to pass out," she said, grabbing an endlessly refilling pitcher from the center of the table and pouring water from it into a lopsided mug. "Take a sip and then tell me what you need."

The water was spring cold and exactly what I needed. I chugged most of the mug and let my brain clear. "Do you remember an incident when you were at Mancer Academy where Delphelius Twench dueled another student and the other student lost an ear?"

Her brows were pinched together, but suddenly her expression bloomed with recognition. "Yes, I do. Goddess, that was years ago! I'd forgotten until now."

"And do you remember the name of the student who lost his ear?" I asked.

She paused. "Oh, I can remember his face. I think he was... No, that can't be right."

"What can't be right?"

"For some reason, I was thinking he was a Bridgewater."

Bingo.

"But it wasn't Levi Bridgewater, and I don't know of another one in town anymore."

"What if I told you there was another Bridgewater but he moved away?"

She narrowed her eyes at me. "What is this about again?"

"Kannin Bridgewater."

"Ah! Yes! He was a South Wind, like me. We had an advanced pyromancy class together my final year. I'd forgotten all about him. He wasn't much of a talker. Sort of stayed out of the way. Very flat affect. Easy to forget, I suppose."

"What if I told you he was back in Eastwind?" I said. "And what if I told you he was posing as a tourist?"

"Sweet baby jackalope," she whispered. "Yes. Yes, of course. Remember when I told you that I thought I recognized some of the tourists? Do you think...?"

"I do. Kannin Bridgewater is here, and I think he killed Delphelius Twench. He won't admit it to me, but maybe you could get him talking. Sheriff Bloom isn't sure how long she'll have the High Council's approval to keep the portal to Avalon shut, and if we can't get a confession out of him, he may be able to go free."

Raven nodded. "This sounds dangerous."

"It probably is."

She breathed deeply. "What kind of a South Wind would I be if that didn't get me a little excited?" She got to her feet. "Okay, I'm in."

* * *

I could see Raven was scared, but you couldn't tell it just by looking at her as she waited by the edge of woods. She'd suggested a meeting place not far from Mancer Academy, where the older students used to meet up away from parental supervision to practice illicit magic, sip whiskey, and try not to get themselves killed.

Would Kannin Bridgewater show up? Maybe, if just for old times' sake, he would.

Atlas and I waited in the shadows, his fur still brown with dried mud, as time ticked by.

The shadows were long, and dusk was starting to settle in. I had faith that the owl Raven had sent out would find the correct recipient, so it was now a matter of whether he would want to come and if he could manage to peel off from the group.

After nearly a half-hour of waiting, as Raven's nerves became slowly visible, another figure emerged from the edge of town, walking toward the tree line. I recognized the red robes and held my breath.

"Raven Goode," he said. "Boy, are you a sight for sore eyes."

"You look just like I remember you, Kannin," she said, and then, to my surprise, offered herself up for a hug. He accepted, stiffly. I felt no genuine affection coming from him, but then again, I felt nothing coming off him, not even small traces of unnameable emotions. Just nothing.

I wondered if this whole thing was a terrible, reckless mistake. Had I dragged Raven into something much more dangerous than either of us knew? After all, if my suspicions were correct, Kannin had killed Delphelius with some sort of fire spell. Raven was a talented witch, no doubt about that, but she'd been using her powers mostly to manage a kiln for the last few decades, not to protect herself from vicious attacks. At least as far as I knew.

They stood in the shadows, taking each other in. "I didn't do what you think I did, you know," said Kannin.

Raven shook her head sadly. "We both know that's not true. But we both also know that you had good reason for it. Del made your life absolute hell for years and years, Kannin. He picked you out as a target and didn't let go. I can only imagine what that does to someone."

"Did you bring me here to comfort me or to force a confession out of me?" he said flatly.

"I came here to help you. I know you killed Delphelius, and I also know that the sheriff has closed the portal between Eastwind and Avalon."

Kannin showed the slightest hint of surprise at the news, but didn't otherwise give away a thing.

"It hasn't been officially announced, so as not to cause a panic among the tourists, but it's true. She

doesn't plan on reopening it until the case is solved."
Raven let that sink in before adding, "You've been
trapped this whole time and didn't even know it. The net
is tightening, and before long, you'll have Bloom's gold
handcuffs around your wrists. Unless you let me help
you."

Kannin glared at her. "Why would you help me?"

"I'd like to say it's because I feel bad for you and
understand why you did it, but it's not that. I hated Del
just like the rest of our class. You left before you could
see what he became."

"I heard a little bit of it from his wife at the pub," he
said. A faint trace of that familiar glee settled on my skin.
"Sounds like he did to her the same thing he did to me."

Raven cocked her head to the side. "The ear?"

"No, not that. The ear is nothing to me. It's what else
he did. The way he looked inside."

I held my breath, wondering what on earth he could
be talking about.

"Looked inside... what?" Raven prompted, anticipation coloring her words.

Kannin leaned toward her, locking with her gaze.
"Looked inside *me*."

Raven's stillness in that moment might've been
confused with bravery, but I knew better; even from this
distance I could feel the ice-cold fear running through
her veins. "What do you mean, he looked inside you?"
she asked.

"The Soul Gaze."

She gasped, a tiny portion of her fear breaking free and escaping. I had no idea what a Soul Gaze was, but it was clearly nothing good.

"He knew how to do that?" she breathed.

"He sure did." There was a hint of satisfaction to Kannin's voice, but I wasn't picking up much else from him. Was he somehow shielding his emotions from me, or did he lack them altogether? "Delphelius learned how to do it his second year at the academy. No idea how, but he did. He was smart in that way, as much as it pains me to give him credit. He used his skill sparingly, though. Didn't run around soul gazing everyone, no. Just used it on key people to maintain status and get them to do as he pleased. I remember the day he did it to me. We were out in the courtyard on our lunch break, and he came up to the table where I was sitting. I was alone, of course, as usual. He sat across from me, and I knew right away that I was in trouble, somehow. I'd seen the way he liked to bully people, and your life would be better if he simply didn't notice you. I didn't want to show him I was scared, though, so I looked him straight in the eye." Kannin clenched his fists, and I waited for the anger to emanate from him, but it simply didn't. "Big mistake. He gazed right into my soul, saw everything that scared me, every secret I'd kept behind my armor, every little thing that could hurt me. Once he locked on, I couldn't pull back. I had to let him keep going, keep mining, keep stripping me of everything I'd locked away until it was all his. All of it. I knew what he intended to do with it, and I was right. He used all of it against me. Day after day, he'd whisper my fears and deep shame into my ears as he passed me in the hallway. He threatened to tell everyone about... about my darkest secrets. He soul gazed me and held me prisoner with it for *years*."

Finally, *finally* I felt it. The rage. A burst of it like a sun flare breaking free. Or perhaps a warning shot. How much of it might still be hidden away below the surface? I didn't want to think about what that much pent-up anger could lead to, what kind of danger I might've asked Raven to put herself in.

Kannin went on. "One day, I got sick of the abuse and stood up to him. I really thought I had a chance to end it. Stupid. I was a stupid kid. Delphelius knew too much about me for any spell I tried to catch him off guard. By then, he knew me better than I even knew myself. I was desperate, though, so I had to try."

Raven nodded slowly. "That's when you lost your ear," she said.

"That was the day, yes."

"I'm so sorry," she said. "I had no idea that was going on. No idea that he held you hostage like that."

"Nobody did. If I told anyone, he'd spread everything he knew about me far and wide, and then it wouldn't just be one person who bullied me, it'd be anyone who got the urge."

"That shouldn't have happened," she said firmly. "Someone should've stepped in."

"Shoulda, coulda, woulda," he said bitterly. "Not

that any of that matters. No one could've done a thing. Besides, I've always suspected Delphelius got to Head-master Typpus. I can't confirm it, but terror recognizes terror. The headmaster couldn't discipline Del because he was under the same threat."

"He could've showed more courage," Raven insisted. "He was a grownup. A full-fledged witch. Surely there was some intervention he ought to have done."

"*You don't get it.* You don't understand what it does to you. When someone like Delphelius soul gazes you, you're done for. You give up. You go numb. It's the only way to keep going. Del's Soul Gaze took *everything* from me. He stole my secrets and fears, and in doing so, he also took my joy, my security, my dreams, and my home. I had to leave Eastwind. I had to start over somewhere no one knew a thing about me, where I didn't have to worry that someone would come along and lay me bare for the vultures to pick at as they pleased.

"I didn't come to Eastwind to kill him," Kannin continued. "At least, I don't think I did. Maybe I had an ulterior motive, but if that's the case, I didn't know about it."

"Then why *did* you come here?" Raven asked.

"I came to revisit my home. You don't know what it's like being so numb for all these years. It keeps you from having your heart ripped out, but it also keeps you from knowing your heart. I was ready to feel again. Truly, that was all I was searching for. I wanted to feel something. And when I stepped inside Sheehan's and saw him sitting there, I felt... nothing. The man who'd taken my life away from me was sitting ten feet from me, and I felt nothing. No hate, no rage, not a thing. Can you even comprehend that? No, of course you can't.

"And then his wife came in, and I saw it in her eyes. I knew immediately that he'd done the same thing to her. He'd soul gazed that poor woman. Maybe even on their first date. And when I thought about that, I felt... Well, I *felt*. I felt for her, even if I couldn't feel for myself. The way she yelled at him; it was like she was speaking for me. The words she said, the emotion in her voice, it broke through the cage I'd put around my heart, and all I could feel was... joy? No, not quite that. I hope you'll forgive me, I'm out of practice with emotions.

"Whatever it was, it was enough. That feeling gave way to a parade of other ones, and I realized that perhaps I'd been away from Eastwind long enough that Delphelius no longer knew everything about me, no longer knew all my pain points. Maybe there were small parts of me that were outside of his grasp now."

Kannin looked like he no longer saw Raven standing right there in front of him. He appeared to be looking through her, lost in some other world.

"I followed him into that alley with one purpose in mind," he said. "I thought about calling his name, to make it a fair fight, but why? Why should I give him a fair fight when I never got one?"

"You killed him when his back was turned?" said Raven.

Kannin grinned. "And when his pants were down, too. I shot fire straight into his heart to stop it instantly. I don't feel one ounce of guilt about that, no matter what you say. Not after everything he did to me, everything he stole from me. At least I made it quick for him. He spent years slowly killing me.

"As soon as he was dead and the connection he'd forged with the Soul Gaze had been severed, I was hit by a repulsive rush. I was free, sure, but emotions I hadn't allowed myself to feel in years sloshed around inside of me, fighting to break free. I stumbled out of the alley and had to vomit. It was like years and years of poison pouring out of me. I thought it might kill me, Raven, I really did. But it didn't. Instead, it gave me back myself. Gave me back my dreams. My desires." He seemed to break from the reverie, and his unfocused gaze suddenly locked on to Raven again. He took a step closer to her. The air around us shifted, but I was slow to catch on to why. "You never knew how I felt about you back then, did you?"

Uh-oh. I looked to Atlas for validation on my foreboding. His hackles were fully raised. He could sense a threat from a mile away.

Kannin might've been a victim all those years ago, but now he was something else as well: a predator. First, he'd killed a man, and now I could see it in the hungry way he was looking at Raven.

She slid back a step, away from him. "I don't know what you mean, Kannin."

"The emotions have been coming in waves since I killed him. No, more than that. Tsunamis. Nothing one minute, then they crash in. I'm not used to them after all these years, and when they hit…" He licked his lips and crept closer to her. She took another step back. "I used to dream about you in school. Del knew it, so I had to shut it off. But he's dead now, and you're here. You came right to me. Almost like it was meant to be. And you know what? I think I deserve to get what I want."

Raven held up her hands, speaking with a firmness I rarely heard from the eccentric potter. "I'm *not* interested, Kannin. I'm sorry."

A devilishness filled his expression, and the palms of his hands glowed like hot coals. "Too bad," he said. And then he lunged for her.

Chapter Seventeen

They were too far from my hiding spot. There was no way I'd reach them before Kannin could overcome Raven.

But I didn't need to. Kannin's emotions had been seeping out slowly as he recalled his harrowing tale, and then the trickle had turned to a flood. All I had to do was take those emotions, gather them, and send them back his way.

I spread my palms and imagined the weight and texture of all those emotions around me, and then I shoved them right back at him.

Kannin was knocked off his feet with a yelp and fell to the ground in a heap just as a massive elk came galloping out of the woods.

About time! I'd been wondering when Stu would've heard enough to intervene!

As the elk changed shape, it was replaced by the familiar form of the deputy in his full uniform. He dropped a knee onto Kannin's stomach and snapped cuffs onto the witch's wrists. The suspect did nothing but blubber—tears streamed down his face from the sudden wave of his own dark emotions reflected back to him, and the words he uttered through the sobs sounded like complete gibberish.

I ran to Raven, who had collapsed onto her backside on the grass. "I'm so sorry," I said. "I shouldn't have asked that of you."

"No, no," she said, waving me off as she stared at the deputy and the killer ahead of her. "I'm glad I did it. All's well that ends well." I didn't quite believe her, but I was happy to let it go for now.

Deputy Manchester recited Kannin's rights to him as he dragged the blubbering witch to his feet. "Twenty tines," Stu muttered. "Pull yourself together. If you think this is bad, wait for Ironhelm Penitentiary."

I helped Raven to her feet, and she dusted herself off and straightened the bun of her purple hair on the top of her head. "That was certainly exciting. I can't wait to tell Jude. He won't believe a word of it, so you might have to back me up."

"It's the least I can do."

"*Umm…*" came Atlas's voice. "*We've got a visitor.*"

I turned toward where my familiar was still hiding in the shadows. A spirit glowed slightly behind him. Delphelius Twench.

"What is it?" Raven asked, catching my sudden shift of attention. "Oh, is he here? Do you see him?"

I nodded.

"I hope you'll excuse me, then. I don't particularly want to be in the presence of that monster, alive or dead, after what I know he's done."

I understood completely. I didn't want to talk to him either.

Raven started off down the slope toward town on her own. I wanted to follow her, to leave Delphelius to his own counsel, but that wasn't how this worked. Besides, if I didn't speak with him now, he might just stick around, and my goal now was to rid this realm of him completely.

"What do you want?" I said, making sure to focus on his forehead as I turned to face him. I wasn't sure if ghosts could pull off a Soul Gaze, but I wasn't willing to find out the hard way.

"Thank you," he said. "Kannin Bridgewater always has been a weasel, and I was the only one who knew it."

"Because you soul gazed him?" I said.

"Exactly. *Somebody* had to. It was obvious he was hiding his weak nature from everyone, and you can't let that go unseen. I gazed him to protect everyone else."

"Swirls!" I spat, feeling a strange rush of anger inside of me. Was that emotion mine or a leftover from Kannin? I leaned toward it being the former.

"Ah, what do you know?" he said dismissively. "You're just a useless Fifth Wind. Can't do real magic, can't solve a murder."

"Can't solve a murder?" I replied. "What do you think I just did?"

He shrugged. "You got lucky."

My annoyance grew. "I won't say *I'm* glad you're dead, but I will say that a lot of people are. Go find Ted. Your tale in Eastwind has been told. It's time to move on, Delphelius."

I put my back to him and walked away, hoping Ted would soon be the last person in town to ever again see Delphelius Twench.

Chapter Eighteen

I was dusting one of the larger vases on display in the shop when the door opened and in walked a face I almost didn't recognize. So changed was she, so much lighter was her step, that I might not have guessed it was Naomi Twench.

The heaviness of old pain still left deep lines around her eyes—a very un-elf-like feature to have—but the pain only looked vestigial, not a current burden.

She looked around somewhat self-consciously as the door closed behind her. It was only me and Atlas in the shop, and perhaps she'd imagined more of a buffer of other people around. After a pause, she headed over to where I stood behind the counter.

"Can I help you find something?" I asked.

"No, no. I'm not here for that." Her voice sounded delicate as a butterfly's wings, much different from the screaming I'd witnessed at the pub and the vitriol she'd spat at the sheriff's department. "I came in because I wanted to thank you. Ted just informed me that Delphelius's ghost has finally moved on." She bowed her head. "I'm sorry I made things so difficult in the interview room. It was tough, you know. It's hard to find the right words when you can't... when you've felt numb for the last thirty years. I didn't want to say the wrong thing and end up in prison for a crime I didn't commit."

"No need to apologize," I said. "I understand."

"You don't, and I'm glad you don't. Delphelius had an ability. One that's forbidden by law, but one he possessed nonetheless."

"The Soul Gaze," I said.

She nodded. "You already know. But what you don't know is what life is like after that. To have no secrets, to have all your pain exposed to someone whose only interest in it is to use it against you. It's horrible. I wanted to leave from the moment we got married, but every time I tried... He knew how to keep me. He knew everything about me. I was trapped. I tried to explain it to others, and they couldn't understand. They couldn't see why I didn't just leave. I ended up sounding crazy, and I knew it. And maybe I *was* a little crazy. If so, he drove me to it."

"I'm so sorry," I said. "That sounds terrible."

"It was. He never worked a day in his life. It was always up to me. I had to clean the house, care for the gardens, run the errands, and work to earn our money. And what did he do? He drank it all away at the pub. He never washed a dish in his life. He threw his clothes everywhere and then yelled at me if I didn't pick them up right away. And when I tried to argue, he would use something he learned from the Soul Gaze against me. I was trapped, not just in my own house, but in my own head. In my own heart. I meant what I said about wanting to thank whoever did this. I'm on my way to the sheriff's department right now to thank Kannin for doing what I couldn't. For freeing me." A tear slipped down her cheek and she quickly wiped it away, staring at the moisture on her finger with something not unlike awe. "All these emotions are new to me again. I couldn't have them before. But I'm free now. Free to cry, free to speak, free to sing, even. And that terrifies me. But I'm sure it will feel normal again at some point." She wiped the tear on her sleeve. "Anyway, I wanted to thank you for finding who did it. I doubt Kannin Bridgewater will ever be my friend, but for now, he's the only person I know who might understand. You've given that to me, and you don't know how much that means." She reached inside her purse and pulled out something shiny, which she slipped across the counter toward me. "A token of appreciation. I... I haven't had any friends since I ran into Delphelius, so I haven't given this out, but we each have one to give. I wanted to offer mine to you."

I held up the shiny white-gold key to inspect it with the sunlight flowing into the shop. "This is beautiful," I said. It was the most ornate key I'd ever seen, with tiny, flowery vines wrapping around it.

"It makes you a friend to all elves. If you should ever

need any help that only an elf can provide, this will let them know that they're obliged to give it. That includes me. And if you ever need to enter Tearnanock, for any reason, that should get you in. I will warn you not to abuse the privilege, though."

"Of course not. Naomi, this is *such* an honor."

My enthusiasm made her uncomfortable, and she withdrew into herself, her emotions receding with her like a sudden low tide. "I'd better get going. Thank you again. It wasn't until I knew his spirit was no longer around that I finally felt... safe. You can't imagine how much of a privilege it is after all these years to feel anything at all. Even the pain feels like a gift."

I watched her go. I might not have understood the torment she'd experienced for so many years, but I was beginning to understand her last point: emotions—all of them—were a gift, even if they didn't always feel that way.

Epilogue

Nora sat on the couch across from me in her living room as I stood, ready. We'd kicked out the familiars to keep their emotions from complicating today's training.

With her eyes shut tight, she brought an image and an emotion to mind. This was our fourth round of practicing this particular skill, and each time, her emotions were weaker than the last. She was clearly still drained from the recent tourism boom, but it seemed like she had things more under control at Medium Rare and had finally managed to get a semi-decent night's sleep.

I tuned in. The emotion hit me first—a subtle one. It wasn't like any we'd attempted before. I tried to pull up the right word, to label the feeling and log it away in my emotional toolbox. It was in the family of happy emotions, but I needed something more specific. Not just happy, but... powerful? Yes, but also more refined than simply powerful.

I caught hold of it and knew instantly. "Courageous," I said.

"Correct. And what's the object?"

Oh, right. I tuned in again. The object took form slowly through a dark haze in my mind's eye, but finally it emerged, shimmering, golden. "Bloom's handcuffs."

Nora opened her eyes. "Correct! You're getting good at this. It's a little freaky. Impressive, but unsettling. I told you that if you put in a little more effort this would be easier."

"You did. And I didn't want to hear it," I said. "A part of me couldn't see the value in feeling everyone else's emotions. It can be overwhelming."

"I can imagine. You used the past tense, though. A part of you *couldn't* see the value. Has that changed?" she asked.

"I suppose it has. I took the power for granted until I met two people who were unable to feel anything at all. Who had shut it all away for years, and to their detriment." A small shiver worked its way down my spine as I thought about the prison both Naomi and Kannin had lived in as a result of Delphelius's Soul Gaze. "Being able to feel everything so precisely like I do is more of a superpower than anything."

Nora chuckled. "I mean, it's a *magical* power, yes."

"Right." I giggled. "I still forget I'm a witch."

"It does take a while to sink in."

I plopped down into a stuffed armchair. "I'm glad we're getting back to training. Partly because that means things are slowing down at Medium Rare for you. You were so stressed out. I was worried about you."

Nora exhaled and dragged a hand down her face. "Things haven't slowed down, exactly, but I did hire more help." She paused. "I brought Jaymes back on."

"Oh. And you're... not worried he'll tamper with someone else's drink?"

"No," she said. "I had a good talk with him about that. He understands that I might give a second chance, but I don't give a third. He needs the job and enjoys waiting tables. I also promised that I'd help him try to reach his mother once the tourism season has ended and I have a little more time, assuming he's on his best behavior." She sighed. "People do bizarre things in grief. He's a strange kid, but I think he has a good heart."

"Me too," I said.

"The poor guy misses his mom. I can't fault him for that. Saying goodbye to someone forever is tough." After a moment of staring off into space, she blinked herself back to reality and slapped the couch cushions next to her. "Again?"

"Sure."

She closed her eyes, and I tuned in. I wasn't sure she was ready yet, though, because all I could sense was the loss she'd been talking about a moment before. I doubted that was the emotion she was trying to conjure for the purposes of our practice, but it was everywhere, lingering like a fog. Emotions tend to hang around like that when we're tired.

In the haze of loss, I spotted a male spirit who bore a striking resemblance to Nora. A brother? Her father? Definitely a story there. The man faded into the ether, and another shape emerged. I recognized this one immediately. But why was Donovan Stringfellow in Nora's head? Why did he appear tangled up in her haze of grief? As he leaned toward me in my mind's eye, grabbing me and pulling me toward him, everything clicked into place, and I jumped back, startled. "Whoa!"

Nora opened her eyes. "What? What happened? Sheesh, I hadn't even settled on an object yet."

I'd seen something I definitely shouldn't have—nothing as intense as a Soul Gaze, but invasive nonetheless. Unlike Delphelius, though, I was determined to forget this bit of Nora's personal history as soon as possible.

"Oh, nothing," I lied, trying to shake off the feeling. "Just got a little dizzy. Hey, I think I'd really like to get better at turning this on... and off. What do you think about increasing our training to twice a week for a while?"

She gave me a suspicious look but finally said, "If you insist."

"I do," I said firmly. "I would feel much better about these powers if I did." ☾

About the Author

Nova Nelson grew up on a steady diet of Agatha Christie novels. She loves the mind candy of cozy mysteries and has been weaving paranormal tales since she first learned handwriting. Those two loves meet in her Eastwind Witches series, and it's about time, if she does say so herself.

When she's not busy writing, she enjoys pottery, talking to plants and eating breakfast for dinner.

Say hello:
nova@novanelson.com

facebook.com/thecozycoven

instagram.com/authornovanelson

bookbub.com/authors/nova-nelson

goodreads.com/nova_nelson

amazon.com/author/novanelson

More books from Eastwind

The Eastwind Witches Cozy Mysteries

Crossing Over Easy (Book 1)

Death Metal (Book 2)

Third Knock the Charm (Book 3)

Queso de los Muertos (Book 4)

Psych-Out (Book 5)

Gone Witch (Book 6)

Love Spells Trouble (Book 7)

Storm A-Brewin' (Book 8)

Hallow's Faire in Love and War (Book 9)

Dead Witch Walking (Book 10)

Old Haunts (Book 11)

First-Realm Problems (Book 12)

Happily Hereafter (Book 13)

The Ruby True Magical Mysteries

Werebear Scare (Book 1)

Elves' Bells (Book 2)

Vampire's Ire (Book 3)

The Dahlia Wildes Magical Mysteries

Time to Kiln (Book 1)

Deadly Inn-Tensions (Book 2)

Throwing Shades (Book 3)

Soul Glaze (Book 4)

Find them here: www.eastwindwitches.com

Printed in the USA
CPSIA information can be obtained
at www.ICGtesting.com
LVHW040115301124
797932LV00003B/515